Ernest J. Gaines

THE TRAGEDY OF BRADY SIMS

Ernest Gaines was born on a plantation in Pointe Coupee Parish near New Roads, Louisiana, which is the Bayonne of all his fictional works. He is writer-in-residence emeritus at the University of Louisiana at Lafayette. In 1993 Gaines received the John D. and Catherine T. MacArthur Foundation Fellowship for his lifetime achievements. In 1996 he was named a Chevalier de l'Ordre des Arts et des Lettres, one of France's highest decorations. He and his wife, Dianne, live in Oscar, Louisiana.

THE TRAGEDY
— *of* —
BRADY SIMS

THE TRAGEDY

—— *of* ——

BRADY SIMS

Ernest J. Gaines

VINTAGE CONTEMPORARIES

Vintage Books

A Division of Penguin Random House LLC

New York

FIRST VINTAGE CONTEMPORARIES EDITION, AUGUST 2017

Copyright © 2017 by Ernest J. Gaines

The Library of Congress Cataloging in Publication data
Names: Gaines, Ernest J., author.
Title: The tragedy of Brady Sims / Ernest J. Gaines.
Description: First Vintage Contemporaries edition. | New York :
Vintage, 2017. | Series: Vintage contemporaries.
Identifiers: LCCN 2017005574 (print) | LCCN 2017012542 (ebook)
Subjects: LCSH: African American men—Fiction. | City and town life—
Fiction. | Race relations—Fiction. | BISAC: FICTION / African American /
General. | FICTION / Literary. | FICTION / Crime.
Classification: LCC PS3557.A355 (ebook) |
LCC PS3557.A355 T73 2017 (print) | DDC 813/.54—dc23
LC record available at https://lccn.loc.gov/2017005574

Vintage Contemporaries Trade Paperback ISBN: 978-0-525-43446-7
eBook ISBN: 978-0-525-43447-4

Book design by Christopher M. Zucker

www.vintagebooks.com

Printed in the United States of America
10 9 8 7 6 5 4 3 2 1

To Wilfred Hebert
   He helps others in so many different ways
      and to
Irwin Mayfield for his "Angola"

Part One

———

LOUIS GUERIN

Chapter One

It was over. We all got up to leave. Two deputies had the prisoner by the arms. I was sitting in back of the court-room because I had been on another assignment and I had gotten there late. I was near the aisle when I heard someone called out loud and clear: "BOY." I looked back over my shoulder and saw that the two deputies had stopped with their prisoner and were facing old Brady Sims. Next came the loudest sound that I had ever heard. I saw the prisoner fall back with blood splashing from his body, and both deputies let go of his arms at the same time. Brady Sims stood there in that old faded blue jumper, with the smoke still rising from the gun in his hand.

Then came the screaming and scrambling to get out of the place or get down on the floor. The members of the jury who didn't run out of the room got down behind their chairs. The judge went under his desk. The two deputies stood frozen, with their hands near their guns, but not on the guns. Brady, facing them—his head as white as cotton is in September—stood as straight and tall as a picket in a fence. I watched him, I watched them all, afraid to run, afraid to get down on the floor.

"Tell Mapes give me two hours," Brady said.

"You don't think you walking out of here, do you?" Claude said. He was the younger of the two deputies.

Brady got his hat off the chair next to the one where he had been sitting. He adjusted it well on that pile of cotton.

"I didn't come here for no foolishness, boy," he said to Claude. "Tell Mapes what I said," he said to Russell, the older deputy.

"Go on," Russell said.

"Go on, like hell go on," Claude said.

Then I heard that deafening sound again—and the smoke rising up between the old man and the two deputies.

"You old bastard, you," Claude screamed. "You tried to kill me, you old bastard, you."

"I shot down in the floor *that* time," Brady told him. "Don't try it no more."

"Go on," Russell said again.

"You crazy?" Claude asked Russell.

"Mapes'll bring him in."

"Mapes put us in charge."

"Go on," Russell told Brady.

"You go'n take the blame for this," Claude told Russell. "By God, you go'n take all the blame for this."

Keeping his eyes on the deputies, old Brady backed his way down the aisle. The two deputies watched him, but did not move. The rest of the people lay quietly on the floor. I watched the old man back closer and closer to where I stood. Then we were facing each other, three or four feet apart. I had known him all my life, but this was as close as I had ever been to him. His face was the color of dark worn leather, and looked just as tough. His mustache and beard were the same color as the hair on his head—snow-white. He had a large hawkish nose, thin lips, and the whites of his eyes were yellow. But those same eyes looked tired and weak.

He continued to stare at me, as if he wanted me to understand what he had done, or why he had done it. But at that moment I couldn't even think, I was barely able to breathe. Still, I couldn't look away.

When he saw no answers in my face, he looked again at the deputies and slowly backed out of the courtroom, with the big gun still in his hand, pointing at nothing.

I took in a deep breath and tapped my chest a couple times to make sure that I was all right, then I went outside.

I saw some of the people who had been inside the courtroom were now standing out on the lawn. Others from nearby stores and shops had joined them. Now, we all watched Brady go to his truck—the big pistol still hanging from his hand. He had to jerk twice on the truck door to get it open. Then he had to back up and go forward twice before he had the old blue pickup straightened out. He drove slowly out of town.

The nearest public telephone was in the drugstore across the street. I ran over there and called the paper. Velma, the secretary, answered. I told her I wanted to speak to Cunningham. Quick. I told him what had happened. He told me to stay there until he got there, and to get everything down that I could. I ran back to the courtroom. The people had gotten up off the floor. The jury members who were left sat in their respective chairs. The judge was sitting at his desk, his hands clasped together as he looked back over the courtroom where a few of the spectators were sitting. The two deputies were standing over the body of the prisoner. Someone had spread a raincoat over the body. Blood flowed from under the raincoat toward the jury box.

Then we heard Mapes. No, we heard the car coming in fast, then screeching to a dead stop in Mapes's parking space. We heard the car door slam and some loud cussing, then he was inside, pushing those two hundred and sixty-nine and a half pounds of fury (he had weighed three hundred pounds a year ago, but his doctor had put him on a strict diet, and he had lost thirty and a half pounds, and he was proud of it, and wanted you to know it). Now he was huffing and puffing and pushing all that weight up the aisle toward us. He looked at his two deputies like he wanted to strangle both of them, then he leaned over and pulled back the raincoat for a second, and flung it back with the same fury. Now he was looking at Russell.

"Out of nowhere—BOOM," Russell said.

Mapes stared at him with those steel-gray eyes.

"Out of nowhere—boom? I'm supposed to tell Victor Jarreau—out of nowhere—boom?"

"Nobody saw it coming," Russell said. "Nobody expected anything like that. He was sitting over there like he's been doing the last two days. Stood up, hollered at the boy, and shot him. What else can I say?"

"You can say you tried to stop him."

"Stop him? Stop him how? Nobody knew what happened 'til it was over."

"He's right," Judge Reynolds said. "I've observed him in that same chair for the last two days. I saw no warning that—"

"You're not paid to see men carrying guns, he is," Mapes said. "Well?"

"What more can I say, Mapes?"

"What more can you say; what more can you say? You can tell Victor Jarreau how this arthritic old man had time to pull out a gun from—I don't know where—time to holler to the boy, time to shoot—while you and this, this thing over here, had your minds somewhere else. Tell him that."

"Mapes," Judge Reynolds said. "I've been sitting here waiting to talk to you, because I thought you could be sensible. But I see it was just a waste of my time. He could do no more to stop Brady from killing that boy than you could have stopped him from wherever you were. Ladies and gentlemen, excuse me, I'll be in my chambers."

The judge left. Mapes was looking at Russell.

"He wants two hours," Russell said.

Mapes was still looking at him.

"Then come and get him," Russell said.

Mapes didn't say anything, but it seemed like those two hundred and sixty-nine and a half pounds of fury wanted to explode.

"Old bastard shot at me," Claude said, out of the quietness.

Mapes heard him, but he went on looking at Russell. Russell had been around long enough to handle situations like these.

"Luckily, the old bastard missed," Claude said, speaking again.

Mapes looked at him this time. He looked at him up and down. He looked at him well.

"He didn't miss," Mapes said. "He don't miss what he shoots at. I've hunted with him enough times to know that he never misses what he shoots at." He turned back to Russell. "Call Herman. Tell him come pick this up. Think you can remember that much?"

Russell didn't answer. Mapes looked down at the raincoat.

"He can have his two hours, then I'll get him."

"Want me to go with you?" Claude asked.

"No," Mapes said. "You've already worked too hard for one day."

"I'd like to be the one to put the cuffs on him, myself," Claude said.

"You can go and arrest him."

"No. Old bastard liable to shoot at me again, and I don't want to have to kill him."

Mapes grunted to himself, then he turned to the jury box where the people sat waiting.

Mr. A. Paul sat in jury chair number eleven. He was the only black member of the jury, a little baldhead man who was a deacon in his church and lived on the same street as I did in Bayonne. He wiped his head with a pocket-handkerchief and stared down at the floor. The white jury members were all looking at Mapes.

"Every last one of you, come to my office," Mapes told them.

"Half of them have already gone," Russell said.

"Find them, round them up, and bring them to my office," Mapes said. He turned to me. "Were you there?"

"Yes, sir, but I didn't see anything, Sheriff."

"Come to my office."

"I swear I didn't see anything, Sheriff."

He didn't say any more.

Just about then Ambrose Cunningham came into the courtroom. All the white people call him Abe or Cunningham. I call him Mr. Abe. He always looks skeptically at me whenever I call him Mr. Abe. He knows I'm laughing inside. He much prefer I call him Mr. Cunningham. But this is the South, and we always address you by your first name. Abe Cunningham is editor of our little weekly, the *Journal.* He is six three or six four, weighs a hundred and seventy pounds at most. He likes his gabardine in winter, his seersucker in summer. He wears a little polka-dotted bow tie all the time. He integrated our little paper about five years ago. A black woman, Velma, is in the office, and I'm a reporter. Jack Richard, a white guy, is the other reporter.

"Mapes," Cunningham spoke, and smiled—something he likes to do whenever he wants information. "Heard you had a little trouble?"

Mapes grunted but didn't say anything.

"May I?" Cunningham asked.

"Suit yourself," Mapes said.

Cunningham pulled the raincoat back and looked at the body, and covered it again.

"Heard he asked for two hours," Cunningham said. "Any comments?"

Mapes noticed that Cunningham had brought out a little tape recorder from inside his coat pocket.

"Talk to your boy over there," Mapes said. He turned to the jury box. "Rest of y'all follow me."

Mapes pushed those two hundred and sixty-nine and a half pounds back down the aisle with the jury members at his heel. There were six or seven of them left; the others ran out of the courtroom when the shooting began. Those left were on Mapes's heel all the way, as though they were afraid Brady might still be around.

"He actually gave him two hours?" Cunningham asked me.

"That's what he said."

"Why?" Cunningham asked.

I shrugged my shoulders. "I don't know."

Cunningham is about three inches taller than I am. He is farsighted and wears thick-lens glasses. His blue eyes behind those glasses looked like bird eggs. I could see in his eyes he was thinking.

"Seems strange to me," he said. "Shoots his son down in a courtroom full of people. Deputies let him go. Sheriff gives him two hours to get his business straight before arresting him—don't that seem strange to you?"

"Like I said, I don't know."

Those two blue eyes looked down on me.

"Go find out."

"Find out what?" I asked.

"You're a reporter, aren't you?"

"I try to be."

"A human interest story on my desk by midnight." He

turned from me to the deputies. "Mind if I ask you boys couple questions?"

"What is it?" Russell asked.

"How did he get in here with that gun?"

"Had it under that old jumper."

"How did he get by security?"

"We don't always check old people, especially the ones we know. How could we know he had a gun with him today?"

"How do you know he didn't have it with him yesterday?"

"You're perfect," Claude said. "I can tell by that rag you publish, you're perfect."

I was standing behind Cunningham, and I could tell by the slight movement of his shoulders that he was laughing at Claude.

"Tell me," Cunningham said. He was speaking to Russell. "From the moment he called to the boy, from the moment the boy fell from your hands, what happened?"

"I better not talk anymore," Russell said.

"Anything to add?" Cunningham asked Claude.

"Go to hell," Claude said.

I could tell by the slight movements of his shoulders that he was laughing at Claude again.

"You boys might need a friend before this is over," he said. He looked back at me. "You're still here?"

Chapter Two

I left the courtroom and went to the sheriff's office. His office was on the same floor, but nearer the entrance to the building. Only two people were still waiting there to see Mapes—juror number ten, a little white lady, wearing a black-and-white checkered suit; and number eleven, Mr. A. Paul Williams. Everyone else had already seen Mapes or had sneaked out while Mapes was in his office. I sat down beside Mr. A. Paul. He had just wiped his face and head with the pocket-handkerchief. He kept it in his hand as though he knew he would need it again. He introduced me to the little white lady. Her legs were so short that her feet barely touched the floor.

"Miss Greta," Mr. A. Paul said.

"Miss Greta."

"Please to meet you," she said. She had rosy cheeks, green eyes, and little red lips.

Juror number six or seven, I forget which, came out of Mapes's office. He was a tall white man with a long neck and orange-color hair. He told Miss Greta that she could go in now. Miss Greta patted Mr. A. Paul twice on the knee just before she stood up. Mr. A. Paul nodded his head and said, "Thank you, ma'am," in response. After Miss Greta had gone into Mapes's office, Mr. A. Paul wiped his face and head again with the wet pocket-handkerchief. He didn't put it in his pocket.

"Nobody never told me jury was go'n cover all of this," he said. "I went through enough of this just to vote. 'How many beans in a jar; how many grains of corn on a cob'—wasn't that enough to make me a citizen? Now this. 'Round here shooting up the place like he's some kind of Jesse James. 'Nough to make you sick."

"Jury duty is not always like this," I told him.

"Ain't it?" Mr. A. Paul challenged me.

"After all, you did sentence his son to death."

"It wasn't just me," Mr. A. Paul said. "It wasn't just me. I went 'long with the rest. So don't go 'round here putting it all on me."

"I was using *you* in the plural sense."

"I don't care what sense you was using it in—just don't go 'round telling people it was just me. I voted like they told me to vote. They all voted the same way. If people had told me jury was go'n be like this, I woulda stayed home."

"It's your civic duty to serve on a jury, Mr. A. Paul."

"Y'all can have all the civic duty y'all want. Just let me stay home and sit in my own chair."

"It's going to be all right, Mr. A. Paul," I said, and patted him on the knee as Miss Greta had done.

"I'm sitting up there, minding my own business, and trying to pay 'tention to what everybody saying—and here he come, shooting up the place."

He wiped his head again.

"Lucky Miss Greta was there," he said. "That white lady saved me."

"Saved you how?"

"Soon's he shot, she hit the floor. She jerked on my pants leg and told me to get down. I landed right on top of her."

"What? You got on top of that white lady?"

"Watch your mouth, boy," he said quickly, and meant it. "I didn't say nothing 'bout getting on top of her. I *landed* on her. *Landed* on her. Now, you just watch your mouth, now."

"You said she got down first, she jerked on your pants leg and you got down on her. With all that floor, you couldn't find any other place to fall?"

"I done told you, boy, watch your mouth," he said, and he was serious. His eyes showed he was deadly serious. "Now, watch your mouth, now."

"Okay, okay, okay," I said. I was grinning inside, but wouldn't dare grin out. "But it must have felt good there for a second. Like falling on a pile of freshly gin cotton."

"Boy, I'm tired, I'm scared, I'm weak," he said, shaking his fist at me. "Now, don't force me to pop you one."

I grinned at him this time. "Okay, Mr. A. Paul, okay. I was just kidding."

"No time to be playing," he said. "My heart ain't that strong."

He relaxed his fist.

Miss Greta came out of Mapes's office and told Mr. A. Paul that he was next. He pushed up from his chair and walked slowly and stiffly and knocked timidly on the door. Mapes commanded him to come in. About ten minutes later he came out and nodded to me to go in. Mapes had just finished drinking a cup of water, and he crushed the paper cup and flipped it over into the waste-paper basket by the clothes rack. His cowboy hat hung on the rack.

"And I suppose you have the same story—you didn't see anything?"

"I told you that in the courtroom, Sheriff."

"Yes you did," Mapes said. "And I didn't believe you then either. Sit down."

I sat in the chair across the desk from him.

"How long had you been there?"

"Maybe half an hour. I got there late."

"You were there half an hour, then what?"

"They had just come in with the verdict. The foreman read it. Guilty. Judge Reynolds spoke to the prisoner couple of minutes. Then the sentence. The chair. The two deputies took the prisoner by the arms. Made a couple of steps. I heard the word 'BOY.' Just, 'BOY.' Then, BAM."

"After that?"

"People were screaming, some getting down on the floor, others were running out of the place. Then another, BAM. I don't want to ever hear that sound again."

"He shot at Claude?"

"I think he shot down into the floor. There was dust and smoke everywhere. I suppose the dust came up from the floor."

"You're sure about that?"

"That's what I saw, Sheriff."

Mapes sat back in his chair, looking over his desk at me.

"Most of them said the same thing. You're sure that all y'all didn't get together to cook up this same story?"

"I didn't get together with anyone. The only person I talked to was Mr. Abe, and I called him on the phone from the drugstore."

"Anyone else out there?" Mapes asked, nodding toward the door.

"I didn't leave anybody else out there."

Mapes leaned forward and pounded his fist on the desk.

"Damn! I hate this."

"Sir?"

"Damn, I hate this," he said. "He's been in and out of this jail as long back as I can remember. My daddy put him in jail, my granddaddy put him in jail, and Guidry had to put him in jail. Now I have to do the same. But this time he's going up for good. Only time he'll come out of Angola again will be in a box. God damn him—why me? Why me?" He pounded his desk again. Then he looked at me as if he was seeing me sitting there for the first time. "What are you doing here?"

"You told me to come to your office, Sheriff."

He continued to look at me as though he was trying to figure me out. We had never spent this much time with each other before. I knew he had watched me, but he never had a reason to question me about anything.

"You're that Guerin boy, ain't you? Samuel and Rachel's grandson? Went away for a while?"

"California—after I finished the eighth grade. I couldn't go to any more school down here and—"

Mapes waved me off. "Yeah, yeah, I know all about that. What brought you back here?"

"I majored in journalism. I wanted to get a job on a newspaper."

"And old good-hearted Ambrose Cunningham gave you that chance?"

"Yes, sir."

"What did you think of the shooting? Enough for a story?"

"Mr. Abe is going to write about the shooting. He wants me to do a profile—a human interest story."

"I thought all of them were human interest," Mapes said. "How's yours going to be different?"

Before I could answer him he had taken a glass and a half bottle of whisky out of the desk drawer. He first blew into the glass before pouring a couple of ounces of whisky into the glass. He downed the drink in one swallow and put the glass and the bottle back into the drawer. He took out a roll of Life Savers, flipped one of the little white round candies into his mouth, threw the rest of the roll back into the drawer, and looked at me.

"Well?"

"He wants to know why you're giving Mr. Brady two hours."

Mapes looked at me. He moved that little piece of candy around in his mouth.

"And when does he want this human interest story?"

"On his desk tonight."

"Tonight?" Mapes was looking at me like he wanted to choke me. "Both you and Ambrose Cunningham are crazy as hell. Both of you ought to be locked up."

"I'm just a reporter, sir. On an assignment."

"I know damn well that Cunningham doesn't know anything about Brady. Do you know anything about him?"

"A little bit."

"A little bit? A little bit?" His hard gray eyes concentrated on me a moment, then he laughed, a short, humorless laugh. "Get out of here. Get out of my office."

"I'm only a cub reporter, sir, and I do the best—"

"Take your cub reporter ass out of my office, and go find that crazy Cunningham and take him to Jackson with you. Get out of here."

"Yes, sir."

Chapter Three

I left the courthouse and drove back of town to Stella's. I asked her for a ham and cheese sandwich. I was still wondering where to go to find that great human interest story. When Stella served me, I asked her. She told me I ought to go to church sometime. I told her that Cunningham wanted the story on his desk tonight, and Sunday would be too late.

"Always in a hurry, huh?" she said.

"Yeah, I guess so."

"Well, I don't know where to— Wait. You ever thought about Felix's barbershop? Always a bunch of liars over there."

"I didn't think about that, but that sounds like a good idea."

When I finished eating I left her a fifty-cent tip—being generous today. Any other time I would have left only a quarter.

Lucas Felix's barbershop was a small square building. Maybe twenty feet by twenty. Lucas had the first chair as you came in, and Sam Hebert had the second. Both Lucas and Sam were in their seventies, and the chairs seemed just as old. The chairs were covered with dark green vinyl, but now all the worn places on the seats, the backs, and the armrests had been patched with black duct tape. The clients didn't mind, because they all were as old as Lucas and Sam and the chairs. There were red, green, and black plastic chairs against the wall for the clients to sit in while waiting to be served. There were a television and a radio on a shelf in one corner of the room, and below the shelf was a drinking fountain. There were pictures everywhere, pictures of Sam and Lucas when they were young men and when they had all their hair. There were pictures of famous athletes like Joe Louis, Jackie Robinson, Muhammad Ali, and Bill Russell. Then there were pictures of Martin Luther King Jr. and the Kennedy brothers Jack and Bobby. And one of Mahalia Jackson singing, and one of Malcolm X preaching, and one of Duke Ellington at the piano. There was also a poster on the wall with the price of haircuts, but the poster had been up there so long that the white paper had turned yellow, and the price of a haircut probably had not changed too much since then.

Most of Lucas Felix's clients were old men, hardly ever any women, and no one younger than I, and I'm twenty-eight. I come there mostly to listen to the old men talk, but I feel that it would be unfair to just sit there and listen and not get a haircut sometimes, so I let Lucas give me an edge 'round the neck every now and then. Other times I go to Jack Bouie a couple blocks farther down the street, who is about my age and gives more modern cuts. At Lucas's barbershop, the old men in there called me youngster. There are always five or six of them in the place from the time Lucas opens at nine o'clock in the morning until he closes at nine at night. Sometimes they are there to get a haircut, but most times just to have a place to come and talk.

I should mention another person who was always there, and that was Sweet Sidney, the shoeshine man. He's in his seventies, maybe eighties. His name was Sidney Green, but everybody called him Sweet Sidney. People my age called him Mr. Sweet. Sweet Sidney was a reader of the *Bayonne Journal*. The *Journal* was only a weekly, but Sweet Sidney read it over and over daily. Whenever you came into the barbershop and he was not shining shoes, you would find him in the client's chair reading the *Journal*. He read the supermarket ads, he read the obituary column, he read the ads on bass and trout fishing. Whenever the other old men couldn't remember a piece of the story, they called on Sweet Sidney. Though he knew the answer, sometimes he would let them wait

awhile before giving it. He knew that he was the intel-
lectual of the barbershop, and they could not get their
information faster anywhere else.

There must have been a half dozen of them sitting in
chairs against the wall. Sweet Sidney as usual was reading the *Journal.* Lucas Felix had a client in his chair, and
Sam Hebert was just finishing up with one.

"Well, youngster, I heard that Brady shot up the
courthouse," Sam Hebert said to me and grinned.

Sam Hebert was a small, thin-faced man with big
teeth. He always had a smile on his face. Always.

"He didn't shoot up the place," I said.

"Not what man on radio said. Man on radio he said he
shot up the place."

Some of the other men looked at me. I was a news
reporter, and maybe I knew things they did not know.
Sweet Sidney went on reading his paper without looking up.

"He shot twice," I said. "He shot his son, and he shot
down in the floor when one of the deputies threatened
him."

" 'Cording to man on radio, Mapes's giving him couple
hours to get his business straight."

"What business Brady got to get straight?" one of the
men sitting against the wall asked.

"Maybe he got to finish that grave?" Jack Shine said.
Jack Shine was a tall, dark-skinned man in his late sixties. He made his living by hunting and fishing and selling his game to a store in Bayonne.

"It was finished," Joe Butler said. "I went back the next day."

"You didn't tell me," Jack Shine said.

"Wait, hold it," Lucas Felix said. "What's this stuff about a grave?"

"Coming back from hunting the other night," Joe Butler said, "we passed by the graveyard. Saw a light. We stopped and looked. We had Clay with us. Scary as he could be. First thing he said: 'Ghost.' Jack said, 'What a ghost doing with a lantern?' Clay took off. Me and Jack got in the cane field to watch. We didn't see Brady 'til he climbed out of the grave. We could hear him knocking the dirt off the shovel. He blew out the lantern. He passed right by us. Lantern in one hand, shovel 'cross his shoulder. Passed right by us. That was the day the trial started for that boy."

"He knowed all the time he was go'n kill him," Frank Jamison said. "He wasn't go'n let his son go to Angola—not as terrible as that place is."

Frank Jamison was a short, dark-skinned man, with a big head, broad shoulders, high butt, and short back. He had just gotten a haircut, and I could see the neat razor edge around the sideburns and on the back of his neck. He had been a salesman for an insurance company, but like all the rest of the men his age he lived on Social Security and a small pension. He sat back in Sam Hebert's barber chair.

"Something like this was bound to happen sooner or later," Jamison said. "The man who whipped children to keep them out of Angola. Some of the old people would rather see their children dead than to go to Angola. 'Cause if they ever came out, they would be dead inside—just broken."

"Educate that youngster, Frank," Lucas said.

Frank Jamison looked at me. He had known me since I was a child. Still he was skeptical of anyone younger than he or better educated than he was.

"Doing something for the paper?" he asked.

"Cunningham wants me to do a human interest story on Mr. Brady."

"What does that entail?"

I could tell that he didn't know what a human interest story was all about, so he had to throw in a word like "entail" that the rest of the people may not have understood.

"Something about his life: the way he lived, his friends, his church—something like that."

"Well, he didn't have too many friends, and he didn't go to church either in his later years. Don't suppose Cunningham wants things like that?"

"If y'all just talk about him, I figure I can find something to write about," I said.

Frank Jamison looked at me suspiciously.

"You think this youngster is all right, Lucas?"

"Sure," Lucas said. "He comes from good stock."

"I know the stock. Been knowing the stock all my life. Him? You think he knows how to listen, and choose, and don't write what he ain't suppose to write?"

"You got my word on it," Lucas said.

"Mine too," Sam Hebert said. "You been to college, been everywhere. You still a Dodger fan, my man?"

" 'Til the day I die."

"Anybody a Dodger fan 'til the day he die is all right with me," Sam Hebert said.

"If y'all say so," Jamison said, still looking at me.

Chapter Four

Nobody said anything for a while. I wanted to ask more questions, but I thought better of it and kept my mouth shut and just listened.

Sweet Sidney turned a sheet of his paper and folded it into fourths; Lucas Felix sitting in his barber chair uncrossed his legs and crossed them again; the client with the new haircut scratched his chin and mumbled something to himself; Jean Lebouef took off his baseball cap and passed the palm of his hand over his bald spot and put the cap back on. Joe Celestin, possibly the oldest person in the barbershop, said, "Yes, yes, yes," to no one but to himself; and nothing else was said until another man came in.

"Gentamans, gentamans," he said.

"Wha's happening there, Tato?" Sam Hebert said.

The rest of the men either mumbled something or made slight gestures with their hands.

His name was Oscar Gray, but everybody called him Tato. He grew watermelons and sweet potatoes on his little farm just outside of Bayonne, and he sold them from the back of his pickup truck on weekends. Since I was a small child I could remember my grandmother sending me to buy sweet potatoes where he had parked by the American Legion hall.

"I s'pose all y'all done heard the news?" Tato said.

"People talking 'bout nothing else," Lucas Felix said.

Tato sat in one of the chairs against the wall. He took off his hat and placed it on his knee.

"Down there at Stella, gittin' me a hot sausage po'boy, when Mapes got the call. He was settin' on a stool down from me, his big butt hanging off both sides of the stool, and he justa watching Stella every move she made."

"Love that brown meat, hanh?" Jean Lebouef said.

"Crazy 'bout it."

"Why don't he just go on and marry her—have her all for himself—hanh?"

"He might be crazy, but he ain't that crazy," Jamison said. "How long you think he'll stay sheriff?"

"'Bout two minutes after them white folks hear 'bout it."

Couple of the old men made a laugh-grunting sound—something like, "hune, huen, ha, uh huh."

"Phone ringed," Tato said. "Stella answered and brought it to Mapes. Old Mapes wouldn't take it right away; he wanted her to hold it 'til he eyed her some more. She smiled at him like she do everybody else—you know that li'l slow, lazy, sexy smile—but old Mapes thinks she do it just for him. He took the phone and said in a quick tough voice, 'YEAH?' And just like that, not even a half a second, his face turned dark, dark red—almost purple. Looked like he had a stroke or a heart attack. One second he was the big lover boy, half a second later he looked like he was dying. Then he started hollering on the phone—'What the . . . ? How the . . . ? Where the . . . ? GODDAMMIT.' He slammed the phone down on the counter and shot out of there. Big's he is, I didn't know he could move that fast.

"Teddy Man was settin' at the other end of the counter. I looked at him, he looked back at me, and we shot out of there to see what was going on. Mapes had already got in his car, was driving a hundred miles a' hour. He was headed uptown, and we figured he was going to the courthouse. Me and Teddy Man started humping it, but I can't pick 'em up and put 'em down like I used to, and Teddy Man can't run any faster either. By the time we got to the courthouse, Mapes had already gone inside. People standing on the grass 'round the flagpole told us how Brady had shot up the place and drove out of town cool as a cucumber. And nobody had tried to stop him or follow him."

It was quiet for a while, until Jamison said: "It was bound to happen, bound to happen. Two hours?"

"That's what he asked for," I said. "And Mapes said he could have his two hours."

"I don't get it," the man with the fresh haircut said.

"So much water under that bridge—eh, Lucas?" Jamison said.

Lucas made a short agreeing grunt.

"Bridge—what—?" the man with the fresh haircut tried to ask.

"When did it get started?" Jamison went on, not paying any attention to the man with the fresh haircut. "Way before I started insurancing. Sometime during the war."

"War?" The man with the fresh haircut tried to speak. "When—war—what war?"

"I say tractor," Joe Celestin said.

Jamison stood there, transfixed, his mouth still open because he was about to say something before old Celestin interrupted him. He stood motionless, quiet, for a couple seconds, then he turned and got a chair from against the wall and placed it in front of the old man and sat down facing him. All of this was done cool and quietly, and everyone else in the place was as quiet as though they were at a wake. Then suddenly Jamison screamed, "WAR, WAR, you old baldhead bastard. WAR."

"TRACTOR, you old wooly head, wooly head—something else," Joe Celestin tried to throw back the insult.

The rest of the men laughed.

The argument between Jamison and Joe Celestin had been going on for years. I had been hearing it ever since I had been coming to the barbershop. Jamison claimed that it was the Second World War that took the young men and women from the plantations to go into the military and to military plants up north for work. Those who went into the military had a chance to go to school to further their education and get good jobs. None of this could have been possible had it not been for the war.

Old Celestin said because the white man had money to buy machines—the tractor—and the black man didn't have the money to buy machines, he couldn't compete with that tractor, and so he had to leave. Old Celestin said the land kept the people together; the city didn't. He said that it made no difference whether it was in the North or down here—city was no school.

"Why don't both of y'all call it draw," Lucas Felix said.

"Lucas, you have been saying that for years, and nothing been solved," Jamison said. "WAR, old bastard."

"TRACTOR, old, old, old nothing."

The men laughed again. But no one laughed harder than Sam Hebert. And I'm sure he had heard the argument a dozen times or more.

"Do you know how precious an education is, old man?" Jamison asked in a controlled voice.

"Do you know how wicked that city is out there?" Joe Celestin asked just as calmly.

"I been out there," Jamison said.

"Me too," the old man said.

"A man is proud when he gets an education," Jamison continued. "Come home with pride. Good food on the table. Can send his children to school. Proud of that."

"And how 'bout all them out on the street?" the old man said. "Ain't trained for any kind of city work. Young ladies got to sell they bodies; young men drinking and on dope, 'cause they can't find any work to do. Eating all that old junky food; half of them skinny as a rail; young ladies fat and bloated up. The land gived them good food, kept them in shape."

"Yeah—picking cotton. No education; pick cotton; cut cane."

"I didn't say nothing 'bout picking no cotton."

"Right, you didn't. Machines doing all of that now. So what's they going to do on the land? Grow a garden—eat potatoes, cabbage, collard greens? All healthy food. But where the money coming from? When they get sick and need a doctor? You can't grow dollar bills in a garden."

"Gov'ment."

"The government? The government? The government gives you just enough money to survive on."

"And I still say—Tractor," old Celestin said. "Done

put poor people in them cities with no kinda training, and they don't know which way to turn. They get in trouble—they end up in the pen or in the grave. Tractor."

Jamison looked at him a moment, then he got up and replaced the chair against the wall.

"You must concede to your elders," he said. "Where was I?"

"Tractor," old Celestin said.

The man with the fresh haircut raised a finger.

"What's that got to do with—"

No one paid him any attention.

"When he first started whipping children," Lucas Felix reminded Jamison. "'Bout the time when Bo-Boy came back from Angola."

"I think you're right—just about that time," Jamison said.

"Called him Bo-Boy because old Alcie Ruffin, his grampa on his mama side, used to stutter, and couldn't get 'boy' out on the first try, so had to say 'bo-boy.' And we all started calling him Bo-Boy. Still don't know what that old boy right name was. You remember, Sweet?"

"Amos Bouie," Sweet Sidney said, without looking up from his paper.

"You're right again there, Sweet," Jamison complimented him. "Old boy could cut cane and pick cotton with the best of them. Lena Jackson could do some picking—"

"Don't forget Vera Domino," one of the old men said.

"Yeah, both of them was right there with him, but no better," Jamison agreed. "Then he got into that trouble, sent to Angola—over what? Poontang. Caught that li'l short-hair woman he used to mess around with with that funny-looking boy from Patin Dike. One punch, and that old boy fell and hit his head on that concrete step, and died two days later. Sent Bo-Boy to Angola for five years. Weighed a good two hundred pounds when they sent him up. When we seen him again—a hundred and thirty pounds at most. Broke, broke, broke. Body and mind—broke. I'm telling the truth, Lucas?"

"I'm a witness."

"Now all he want to do is chew sugarcane and eat pecans," Jamison went on. "Go back in the field and break a whole armful of cane, sit on that ditch bank front of the house and peel cane with them few old rotten teeth he still had and chew on sugarcane all day long. Go back under them pecan trees, stuff pecans in his overall and jumper pockets, come back, set on ditch bank front of his house and eat pecans 'til Aunt Ducy got to come out in the dark and lead him back to the house. People keep telling her she ought to take him to Jackson, but she keep telling them he ain't hurting anybody, and that she could take care of him all by herself."

Jamison was quiet for a moment. Joe Celestin got up and went to the bathroom. The man with the fresh haircut went to the fountain to get some water. He wiped his mouth with the back of his hand and sat down in the chair next to me.

"You follow what's going on?" he whispered in my ear.

I nodded.

"Must be some kinda secret code in this part of Louisiana."

I caught a whiff of the lotion that Lucas Felix had put around his neck after cutting his hair.

"Who was preaching then, Lucas?" Jamison asked.

"Better ask the man there," Lucas said.

"Hanh, Sweet?"

"When?"

"The War—when it was just getting started?"

"Tractor," old Celestin said, coming out of the bathroom.

Sam Hebert laughed.

"Tyree," Sweet Sidney said. "Banks came after the war."

"You're sure?" Jamison asked.

Sweet Sidney didn't say another word. Take it or leave it.

The fellow with a fresh haircut made a clicking sound as if he was trying to get something from between his teeth.

"Yeah—right—Tyree," Jamison said. "Big, healthy fellow—black as tar."

"When's he going to say something about the boy

who was killed?" the fellow beside me whispered. Again, I could smell the lotion around his neck. I didn't answer him.

Jamison went on: "One Sunday after church service, Tyree told the people not to leave just yet. He had been getting complaints about children the old people couldn't control. The mamas and the papas had gone to war or up north for work, leaving the children with the old people. Now, the children stayed in trouble. Always going to jail; some going to Angola. They brought up Bo-Boy for an example what happened when they went to Angola. And they didn't want to see that happening to their children. They wanted Tyree to tell them what to do. Tyree told them that if they couldn't control the children—get somebody on the place who could. But who? Then they came up with Brady. Brady Sims. Brady could stop them. None of Brady's kids ever got into trouble. Brady was the man to do the job. They went to Brady. Brady said if that's what they wanted. They said that's what they wanted. And they warned their children: 'Keep it up, keep it up, just keep it up. You'll meet with Mr. Brady whip. You just keep getting in trouble.'"

Jamison looked back at Lucas Felix.

"You still with me, Lucas? You mighty quiet in that chair."

"I'm with you all the way, man," Lucas Felix said. "You got it to a T."

"I wish I knowed what's he talking about," the fresh haircut man said to himself, but loud enough for me to hear.

"First one he had to whip on the place was Aunt Tobias's old lazy grandson, Nelson. Mon and Pa had gone to California for work. Aunt Tobias could hardly move around with her walking stick, and now she had this old boy on her hands. Old boy would steal a nickel off a dead man's eye. Stole that dollar that Lizzy Ann wanted to send to her sister, Irene, on the Island. Time was hard then, time was hard for poor people. If you didn't make a garden, and you didn't have a few chickens, a hog, or a cow, you saw some hard days. I was selling insurance then—had that stretch from Gross Stete to Mulatto Bend, and over on the Island. I was on the Island when Irene told me to tell Lizzy Ann to please send her two dollars for medicine the doctor had told her she had to have. I didn't collect the quarter that day, she didn't have it.

"When I came back on this side of the river I told Lizzy Ann what Irene had said. She said she couldn't spare two dollars, but maybe she could scrape up one. She asked me when I was going back on the Island. I told her not for another week. She said she would try to mail it. She asked me if I had a stamp. I didn't have one on me, but I gave her a nickel. Stamps cost three cents at that time. She put the old wrinkled dollar bill in the envelope with another piece of paper so you couldn't see the money. She asked me to write the address because I wrote so much better than she did. Then she got that old boy Nelson to mail the letter for her. She gave the old boy the envelope and the nickel for the stamp, and she told him he could buy some candy with the two pennies left over. At that time you could buy those little penny sticks of peppermint candy. Old boy tore open that envelope, took that dollar, bought him some sausage and moon cakes and a bottle of pop, and sat under that pecan tree—at that time you had a big pecan tree right by the store—he set there with his legs crossed and had himself a feast. People visiting the store saw him sitting there. Some of them asked him where did he get the money from. He told them that it was none their business. He told other people that he found it in the road.

"Three, four days later, I went back on the Island. Irene asked me if I had spoke to Lizzy Ann. I told her that Lizzy Ann couldn't send her two dollars, but could send her one. Irene said she never seen any money. When I came back on this side I told Lizzy Ann. Lizzy Ann went to Aunt Tobias. Aunt Tobias was too weak to catch and whip Nelson, so she went to Brady. When Brady finished with him Aunt Tobias had to bathe his back in Epsom salt water for a week. That old boy saved up enough money to visit his folks in California. Aunt Tobias died not long after that, and Nelson and his mon and pa came back for the funeral. When Nelson got up to speak, he thank Brady for changing his life. He thank him over and over. You was at the funeral, Lucas, am I right or wrong?"

"Right—every word."

Jamison got some water from the fountain and wiped his mouth with the back of his hand.

"I was on my way to N'Awlens," the man with the fresh haircut whispered in my ear. I got a faint whiff of the lotion. "When's he go'n get to the part—where the boy was killed?"

I didn't answer him.

"Yep," Jean Lebouef said to himself and laughed. "Saved some, lost some; and sometimes it was just funny. Settin' here thinking 'bout the time Brady tried to whip P.J."

Several of the men laughed, Sam Hebert was one of them. He laughed harder than anyone else.

"That was some day, that was some day—I tell you," one of the other old men, Jake Williams, said.

Jamison sat in Sam Hebert's barber chair, crossed his legs, and started talking again.

"Old boy stayed hungry," he said. "Dinnertime, he could eat a half a pound of sausage and a half loaf bread without stopping."

"Now, he could pick some cotton, though," one of the old men said.

"You telling me," Jake Williams said. "Up there with the best of them."

"And stole cotton out of other people sacks out on the headland," Jean Lebouef said.

"He the one he killed?" the man with the fresh haircut asked me.

I didn't answer him.

"But when it rained, you couldn't pick cotton," Jamison went on. "Old boy missed that half loaf of bread and that half pound of baloney sausage, so he stole it. Went out to the store, and when old Billy Boudreau was on the telephone back in his office, that old boy leapt over that counter and grabbed a hunk of sausage, and leapt back over and grabbed a loaf of French bread and a couple bottles of pop, and headed for the quarter. He knowed all the time that they was going to find out who did it, so he got some bricks and broke them up in chunks, and he took food and bricks under the house and started eating and waiting. Big old boy, nineteen or twenty. Who was his paw? Sweet?"

"Louis Paul," Sweet Sidney said, without looking up from his paper.

"Yeah, right," Jamison agreed. "Did favor them Pauls from Loddio. All of them, big fellows, always in trouble. Couple of them even served time in Angola."

"Wait, wait, wait," I heard behind me. "You say you follow what he's talking 'bout? You sure you work for a newspaper—the paper that fellow over there can't stop reading? Positive?"

I ignored him.

Jamison never stopped talking. "Cousin Mama 'Nita who was raising him was going to keep him out of Angola no matter what it cost. And that's when Brady comes in. Had rained that day—won't never forget. Ground soaking wet. Brady had to get down on his stomach to look under the house. Was dark way under there, but Brady could make him out. Him under there still eating that French bread and baloney sausage. Brady had that whip, that eight-plat bullwhip. He popped under there—po'yow. Old boy went on eating his bread and sausage.

" 'Come out from under there,' Brady told him. 'Don't make me have to come and drag you from under there.'

"Old boy went on eating his bread and sausage and drinking his pop—Nehi. He knowed he was out of reach of Brady's whip. Brady musta swung under there three or four times, but it never come anywhere near that old boy.

"A lot of people had gathered now, standing there on that wet grass watching this. I reckoned half of them was pulling for Brady, the other half for P.J. Brady started crawling under the house, and that's when that old boy throwed that first brick. It missed. Brady stopped a second, then started crawling again. That second one didn't miss, caught Brady on the arm. You remember all them Pauls used to play baseball. We had baseball parks then—one here, another one at Caledonia, Port Allen, the Island—everywhere. Those was the good old days. And them Pauls, all of them, was good. Skee-ter played shortstop, Juney was on second, the rest was either pitchers or in the outfield. All good. Coulda gone to the majors if they had good training. All big healthy boys—strong arms. You with me, Lucas?"

"All the way," Lucas Felix said.

"Why the barber keep agreeing with him?" I heard behind me. "Can't he see that man's crazy? You sure he didn't break out of Jackson?"

Jamison went on talking. "That second brick made Brady back off from under the house. He pretended he was going to leave, then he went tippy-toeing to the other side of the house. By the time he got down on his stomach, that old boy had changed sides, too, holding on to his food and his Nehi pop and a couple of bricks. The rest of the people went to that side, too, just to see what was going to happen. Brady popped that whip under there couple times, then he tried to rush that old boy. The first brick hit him on the arm, the second brick right square on the forehead. Brady just laid there, laid there, 'til couple men grabbed holt of his legs and pulled him out. Jake, you was one?"

"Me and Ned Brooks," Jake Williams said.

"Brady had nothing else to do with P.J., and P.J. had nothing else to do with Brady. Old Boy went to Texas, stayed there a while, then went to California. Was mur-dered there in Oakland, California, in a bar fight."

"Leaving home, going to them streets—dying," old Celestin said.

"They're dying here, too—or haven't you notice that?" Jamison said.

"Tractor," old Celestin said.

The old men were quiet for a while. So was I. But I was still waiting for something else. What was the meaning of those two hours?

Chapter Five

_____

Two other men came into the barbershop—Lloyd Zeno
and Will Ferdinand—both farmers. They wore country
clothes—khakis and denim.

"Hub-hub," Will said, and sat in Lucas's barber chair.

"Gentlemen," Lloyd said. He pulled out a chair from
the table where the men played checkers. He didn't need
a haircut.

Jamison was still sitting in Sam Hebert's barber chair,
and Sam was leaning on the back of the chair.

"Eula took them children away from here—when—
just after the war?" Jamison asked.

"Tractor," old Celestin said.

"Still at it?" Lloyd asked.

"Every time," someone said.

"Does it matter?" I heard the man with the fresh haircut behind me say. "Tractor, war; war, tractor—does it matter? . . . That big Creole woman go'n kill me for sure—go'n kill me. . . . Why did I have to stop here for a haircut? Coulda got one in Natchitoches—cheaper. Ever been to Natchitoches?"

I shook my head. I wanted him to leave, and I didn't want him to leave.

"From here, you hit I-90, and swing right. Go west 'til you see the Alexandria turnoff—that takes you to 49. 49 takes you straight to Natchitoches—two and a half hours—can't miss it."

"That boy—Charlie—how Brady beat him—helped her make up her mind to leave here," Jean Lebouef said.

"Over that bicycle," Will Ferdinand said.

"Is he the one?" I heard behind me.

I didn't answer him.

"LeDoux used to put things out on the sidewalk for people to see. That's how he advertise his store—things out on the sidewalk. Garden and field stuff. But that day, he had that bicycle out there with all the rest of his things. Pretty, shiny red-and-white bicycle—a Schwinn. That old boy jumped on that bicycle, headed for home. One of Mapes's deputies caught up with him about half-way. Mapes called old Billy Boudreau and told him to get somebody to go tell Brady that he had his boy in jail. Brady didn't have a truck then, and got Sam Brown to take him to Bayonne. Brady told Mapes he wanted to be in that cell five minutes with his boy. Mapes had seen that big belt around Brady's waist, but he thought Brady would just talk to the boy in the cell, and beat him when he got outside. No. Brady started in the cell, hitting the boy across his back and his head with the buckle end of the belt. The boy went down on the floor, Brady continue to beat him. Mapes rush into the cell cussing—'You ain't go'n kill him here in my jail; kill him somewhere else.' He grabbed Brady and pushed him back, and he helped the boy up off the floor. Brady raised the belt to hit Mapes, and Mapes told him that would be the last time he ever raised that arm. He pushed Brady and the boy out of the cell. 'Kill him somewhere else,' he said. 'Then I'll come for you.'

"Sam Brown said Brady threw the boy in the backseat and got in there with him and started beating him again. Halfway home Sam Brown said he told Brady he was going to stop the car and they had to get out. Brady told him if he stopped that car he was go'n use that belt on him. Sam Brown said he said to himself: 'In all the years I've been carrying my gun, I had to leave it home today.' When he stopped in front of Brady's house, Brady opened the door and pushed the boy out. The boy fell to the ground. Brady said, 'How much I owe you?' Sam Brown told him a dollar.

"Brady said, 'A whole dollar?' Brady said, 'You said it was go'n be fifty cents to take me there and bring me

back. You go'n charge a whole fifty cents just to bring
him back?' 'You see all that blood on that seat back
there?' Sam Brown asked him. Brady said, 'Yo car; clean
it up if you want to. Here's yo seventy-five cents.'

"Brady grabbed the boy by the collar of his shirt and
started dragging him to the house. Sam Brown said he
looked at the fifty-cent piece and the quarter, and looked
at Brady dragging the boy up the steps, and dragging him
into the house. He said he said to himself, 'I know there
is a God. It was all God's doing, making me leave that
gun at home. They say He works in mysterious ways. I
believe it.'"

Jamison left the barber chair and went to the toilet.
The room remained quiet, except every now and then
one of the old men would say something to himself. I
could hear the snip, snip, snip of the scissors Lucas used
cutting his client's hair.

"What's the matter with the rest of these old fellows?" I heard behind me. "He's the only one who know
what happened? . . . That li'l fellow over there—he ever
look up from that paper? I don't think he's turned that
page once. . . . Lord, have mercy, why am I still here?—
Why? . . . You ever knowed a big Creole woman?"

I shook my head.

"You doan know what you been missing, partner.
Cook. Dance. And get you in that bed—oh, Lord . . .
Sure you never knowed one?"

I shook my head.

"I kinda like you—I'll find you one. . . . You think I'm crazy?"

I shook my head.

"I think I'm crazy. Sitting here, knowing what's waiting for me in N'Awlens—and I'm sitting here listening to this shit. When I leave here I ought to drive myself straight to Jackson and tell them to lock me up please."

Jamison came out of the toilet, got himself some water from the fountain, and sat back in the barber chair.

"Now, I can't remember what I was saying."

"Brady beating Charlie over that bicycle."

"Oh yeah, yeah, yeah," Jamison said, making himself comfortable in the chair. "Them two oldest boys, Harry and Marshall, had volunteered for the service just to get away from Brady. Even in their teens, Brady was still beating them when they did something wrong. He swore no child of his was going to Angola—he would kill them first. The boys used to send money to their uncle over there at Pitcher to give Eula when she needed it. They wouldn't send it directly to her for fear Brady would get his hands on the money before she did. They told their uncle Claiborne to tell her to get away from that house, her and the children, the first chance they got.

"Brady used to go deer hunting with Mapes and some other white fellers from Baton Rouge. Had a camp over there in Mississippi—a big cabin—all slept in the same cabin—even Brady. Stayed two, three—sometimes four days. They left that Friday. When Eula thought Brady was gone for good, she gave one of the children fifty cents and told him to go see Brown. Sam Brown told her nope, because he didn't want to have to kill Brady. Eula told two of her children to get on the horse and go to Pitcher and tell her brother Claiborne she was already packing. Claiborne brought the children back in the truck, and by midnight they had finished packing and was leaving. They first went to Texas—Houston—she had people there. From Texas she went to California, where Marshall was stationed. He was married—had children— Eula and her children stayed with them.

"Brady came back about ten that Tuesday morning. The plantation was quiet, quiet. Doors and windows shut tight. Only one person out on the gallery—Sam Brown—with his shotgun 'cross his lap. He saw Mapes drive by with Brady, saw him help Brady carry his tub of deer meat to his gallery, and watch him drive back by. Mapes touched the horn, Sam Brown waved a finger.

"Now, usually, the old people would send one of the children down to Brady when he came back from hunting, 'cause Brady gave most of that stuff away. Just about everybody could get a piece of meat if they wanted it. But not that day. Nobody showed up. No doors opened. No windows opened.

"Then they heard him. 'EULO, EULO, EULO. Where is you, woman?'

"He shot up in the air—POW, POW. 'EULO, where is you, woman? Come to me, woman. EULOOOO.' He didn't sound like a man—more like a' animal—a were-wolf. Calling her name, and shooting up in the air.

"Then he was standing in front of Sam Brown's house.

"Sam Brown, with his gun across his lap, told Brady, 'Don't come in this yard with that gun, Brady. You want talk to me, talk to me out in the road. Or you can leave that gun out there, and come in here. But don't cross that ditch with that gun.'

"Sam Brown had his finger near the trigger of his own gun.

"'You took her and them chillen 'way from here?'

"'No,' Sam Brown told him.

"'You seen who took them 'way from here?'

"'Yes.'

"'Who?'

"'Find out for yourself. Just don't cross that ditch with that gun.'

"'Somebody in the quarter?'

"'Find out for yourself.'

"'Them from Pitcher?'

"'Find out for yourself.'

"Brady looked left, he looked right. Nobody was on the gallery. Doors and windows shut tight.

"Sam Brown said Brady threw his head back and cried up to the sky—'EULOOOO, EULOOOO, where is you, woman? Where my chillen at?'"

Chapter Six

———

"Think if I call her and tell her I had a flat tire she'll believe me?"

I nodded.

"I don't know, I just don't know," he said. "I told her that before—gambling there in LaPlace all night, 'til morning. . . . I don't know. Maybe I could tell her the car broke down—always having some kind of trouble with that old car. Think that'll work?"

I nodded.

"I don't know. . . . Man, I wish I hadn't stop by here for no haircut. Anywhere but here—anywhere . . . Think he'll let me use his phone?"

I nodded.

"You sure?"

I nodded again.

He got up from the chair and went over to Lucas Felix.

"Local or long distance?" Lucas asked.

"N'Awlens."

"You can use it. Don't stay on too long."

He turned his back to us as he dialed the number. She must have been sitting near the phone. He spoke quietly as he could. The shop was silent, not to listen to his conversation, but to give him privacy. We could still hear him.

"Honeybun, honeybun—sound like you mad already. Honeybun, listen; please listen; the car broke down on me. Honeybun—now, you don't have to cuss like that."

Sam Hebert was laughing so hard to himself, he had to go to the bathroom. I could hear him in there clearing his throat.

The fellow was saying: "I been trying to fix that old car last two hours. . . . I'm talking low 'cause other people in the room. . . . Honeybun, please, please . . . Bayonne—Bayonne, a little town between Opelousas and Baton Rouge—St. Raphael Parish—you can find it on the map. . . . No, no, honeybun, now, I know you don't mean what you just said. God in heaven knows you don't mean what you just said. . . ."

Sam Hebert started out of the bathroom, shook his head, and he went back inside. He couldn't stop laughing.

The fellow on the phone was saying: "I worked, I

worked, and I worked on that old car. A fellow brought
me here so I could use the phone. First thing I did
when I got here was call you to tell you not to worry,
'cause I know how much you worry when I drive from
Natchitoches to N'Awlens in that old car. I didn't want
you to think I had been in a wreck and— Honeybun,
you know you don't mean that, that you wished I had
been in a wreck and was dead.... There ain't no woman
here. This a barbershop. You want speak to the barber? You don't have to say that, honeybun, this a nice
man, let me use his phone to call you.... I ain't go'n stay
with the barber. Soon's I get that old car fixed, I'll be
there to take you to Dooky Chase.... You'll already be
there with who? That nigger with all that cheap-ass
gold in his mouth? You wearing what? That pretty
green dress I bought for you for Christmas. Shit—I'm
mad now ... and coming there.... He carry a gun, huh?
I carry one, too. And tell that nigger he better shoot
straight, 'cause I don't miss. That nigger too ugly to take
anything from me—'specially my woman. See you later."

He hung up the phone.

"How much I owe you, sir?" he asked Lucas.

"Nothing," Lucas said. "You have enough troubles."

"Excuse me, gentlemen," he said.

He went to the bathroom as Sam Hebert was coming
out wiping his eyes. He was in there about five minutes.
When he came out he sat beside me again.

"Sorry, man," I heard him whisper. "Sorry I had to lie

to that woman like that. He's the cause of it, he caused it. He knows he had me hooked from the start. They do that. Start telling you a story and they know you won't leave 'til you heard the end. You understand what I'm saying?"

I nodded.

"Got you hooked, too?"

I nodded again.

"They do it on purpose—hook you like that? On purpose. I hope one day I can catch him up in Natchitoches. Don't y'all ever get tired listening to that jackass?"

I didn't answer him, I was listening to Jamison:

"Not long after Eula took them children and left him, he started going with Mika Leblanc from Chenal. He had a tiger on his hand. He slap her, she hit him back with her fist. He hit her with his fist, she hit him back with a piece of stove wood. Back and forth, back and forth, 'til she left. Next was Lettie White, a little Creole woman from Livonia. Stayed with Brady about six months, then she went back to her own people. Then he took up with Betty Mae. Y'all still with me, Lucas? You pretty quiet there."

Lucas Felix assured him that he was with him all the way. Others told him that he was telling it like it was.

With their approval, Jamison went on:

"Had two children by him, a girl and a boy. The girl was pretty, pretty like her mama. Had that tan, creamy color like Lena Horne. The boy was darker—more chocolaty—and ways just like Brady—stayed in trouble. Brady used to beat him, but that didn't do no good. Boy had too much of Brady's blood in him.

"Brady was getting up in age, in them late sixties or even in his seventies. Couldn't whip like he used to. Now he had to pick up a chunk of wood or a brick to throw at Jean-Pierre. One day he gave Jean-Pierre the shotgun and two shells and told him to go out and get a rabbit for supper."

Sam Hebert laughed. Some of the others did, too, but kept their laughter to themselves. The laughing didn't stop Jamison:

"Jean-Pierre came back a' hour later—no rabbit. Brady told him with all those rabbits running 'round in the fields, he couldn't get one rabbit? Jean-Pierre told him he couldn't get one. Brady told him to give him back the gun and the bullets. Jean-Pierre handed him the rifle and told him that he had shot at two rabbits but had missed. Brady said to Jean-Pierre, 'You mean to tell me you shot two whole bullets and missed hitting one rabbit?' Jean-Pierre said, 'Yes, sir.' Brady told him to wait, he was going to get just one bullet and see what he could hit. Jean-Pierre bust out of the house, headed for the field. Brady shot, 'pow,' hitting a corn stalk on a row next to where Jean-Pierre was running. He hollered at Jean-Pierre he better bring a rabbit to that house for supper or don't come back to the house.

"Teddy Man had been hunting that day. On his way

back home he saw Jean-Pierre sitting under a tree on that back road. He was crying, his shirt soaking wet from running. Teddy Man asked him what was the matter. Jean-Pierre told him. Teddy Man had three or four rabbits in a sack. He dropped the sack, reached in, got one of the rabbits, and gave it to Jean-Pierre.

"Not long after that, Betty Mae left Brady and took her children to N'Awlens. In N'Awlens, she took up with Lena Aguillard's oldest boy, Phillip. Phillip used to send Lena a few dollars every so often, and she was always bragging on him, saying how he was making something of himself. He told her that him and Betty Mae and the girl got along very well, but Jean-Pierre stayed in trouble, and they were always bailing him out of jail. In another letter he told her that he had heard there was a lot of work out in California, and Betty Mae thought they should go so she could get Jean-Pierre out of N'Awlens. In his next letter, a month later or two months later, he told her that they had settled down in a little town called Valley Jo, and both him and Betty Mae had gotten good jobs in another little place called Mare Island, just across a little body of water from Valley Jo. The girl was in junior college, but Jean-Pierre still stayed in trouble. Now he was running 'round with a gang and he was smoking dope.

"By now Brady had taken up with Dorothy Lee Brooks. Her husband, Sidney, had died the year before."

"My God—just look at the time—" I heard behind me.

"When Sidney died, Dorothy Lee was left by herself

to take care that old lazy Norman. Boy wouldn't work for nothing. Stayed drunk. First thing every morning he walked down to that corner store and buy a bottle of that old cheap muscatel wine from Te Jacques. Dorothy Lee begged Te Jacques not to sell him no more wine. Te Jacques told her, what was he in the business for but to please his customers—hanh? 'Long as he brings his money, I have to sell it to him. I don't let him have it on credit. But with money—*mais oui.*' Dorothy Lee went to Mapes. Mapes told her he couldn't tell Te Jacques who he could or couldn't sell his goods to. And he couldn't tell Norman anything unless he broke some kind of law. So far he hadn't. Now, she told Brady when they started seeing each other. Norman played it cool for two or three days, then he just had to have that wine. Cut grass all day with nothing but a yo-yo blade. When he finished, that old white woman, Slim Jarreau's old mother-in-law, gave him one dollar—enough to get a half pint of that old cheap muscatel wine. First thing next morning he headed out for Te Jacques. Brady let him get a good head start, then he followed with that eight-plat bullwhip 'cross his shoulder. He waited across the road for Norman to come outside. You see, you could buy the liquor in the store up front, but if you wanted to drink it, you had to go outside or go to that little side room they called the nigger room.

"White people could drink in the front where they bought grocery, but you couldn't. And old Norman wanted a drink soon as his hand hit that bottle. He

opened that door and went outside and took a big swallow. He raised that bottle to get another swallow, and
that's when he spotted Brady. Brady started toward him,
Norman took a quick swallow and started walking in
the center of the road. That's when Harry Chutz's boy
came around the bend in that pickup truck and hit him.
Ronald, that big redhead boy, said he did everything he
could to stop that truck, but he was going too fast to stop.
He got out of the truck crying, saying, 'I did all I could
to stop. God knows I did all I could to stop. But he was
in the middle of the road.' They took Norman to the
hospital. He was crippled, not dead. Maybe all that wine
in him saved him. They took both Ronald and Brady
to jail. But after the judge heard what he had to say—
and Brady backed him up—the judge let him go. Mapes
spoke up for Brady—how Brady tried to keep children
in line when the old people could not. Reynolds, Judge
Reynolds, told Brady he knew about him, how he had
helped the older people with the children while mon
and pa was away—but still he ought to lighten up. He let
him go. Few days later Norman came out of the hospital
on crutches. Still on crutches to this day. No more Te
Jacques though.

"Brady was getting older, getting older, and he moved
out of the quarter back into the field—in that same old
house he had lived in years before—by the old sugarhouse. Before he could move in he had to run possums,
snakes, rats—every kind of vermin you can think of—

out of the old house. House had lost couple of blocks, making the gallery lean to one side. That didn't bother Brady—he just wanted to get away from those 'quarter niggers.'

"He got one of them Jarreau boys to plow up enough ground to make a garden. He planted watermelons, mushmelons, snap beans, okra, tomatoes, cucumber—anything you can name, he had it. He got Will Bergeron to sell him that old truck for fifty dollars. Old truck had been setting there idle for the longest.

"Brady used to pack his gardening on that old truck and go park 'side the highway. Stay there 'til late in the evening, then come on back home. People coming in from hunting would pass by his house and see him setting on the gallery smoking his pipe. The only person he let visit him was Noah—hanh, Noah?"

Noah was a small man with a patch of hair up front, bald in the middle, and hair on the sides and back of his head. He was a widower, and for company he spent as much time at the barbershop as he did at his own home.

"I'm a Christian man—" he said.

Next to my ear I heard, "Shit, now I got to listen to a goddamn sermon."

"And being a Christian, I feel that no matter how much a man thinks he wants to be by himself, he wants li'l company every now and then. I thought it was my Christian duty to visit him, even if he told me not to come in—being a Christian I had to try. He was set-

ting on the garry in a rockin' chair—one of them straw-
bottom rockin' chairs. I spoke, he spoke back.

"I started to sit down on one of the steps, but he told
me to come on up. And he went inside and got another
one of them straw-bottom rockin' chairs. We set there
maybe couple hours, talkin' li'l bit; quiet awhile; talk li'l
bit mo'; quiet li'l bit mo'. Went on like that for 'bout couple hours; then I told him good night.

"Next time I went by, he told me to come on up. We
just set and talk, talk about anything. He always planted
more than he could eat or sell. Used to give me sacks of
stuff to give people in the quarter. Didn't mind giving
them food, but don't bother him. No more hunting, eyes
had gone bad; but he liked his gardening. Just like to see
things grow that he planted. Sometimes we just set there
a long time, not saying a word.

"He musta been living back in the field two, maybe
three years when that boy—Jean-Pierre—came back."

"That's the one he's goin' to kill?"

I nodded my head.

"Finally," I heard behind me.

"'Most sundown. If you looked 'cross the sugarhouse,
you could see that sun slipping behind the trees. I could
see that dust following that car in the quarter about a
mile away. Then the car come up and stopped in front of
the house. That boy looked at us awhile 'fore he got out
and come in the yard.

"'This my daddy's house?'

" ' 'Pending on who you looking for?'

" 'My daddy, Brady Sims.'

" 'Come on up,' I told him. 'That's him sitting right there.'

"He stopped in front of Brady and stuck out his hand. Brady didn't offer his.

" 'Hi, Daddy,' he said.

" 'Who you?' Brady said, looking up at him.

" 'Your son, Jean-Pierre.'

" 'I don't know no Jean-Pierre.'

" 'Betty Mae son.'

" 'I don't 'member no Betty Mae.'

"The boy looked at me, then back to Brady.

" 'You shot at me once.'

" 'I missed?'

" 'Yes, sir, and I'm glad you did.'

" 'I don't 'member that. What you want?'

" 'I come to find my daddy.'

" 'You running 'way from the law, boy?'

" 'Of course not.'

" 'You running 'way from something.'

" 'I'm not running from nothing. I just wanted to see my daddy.'

"He stuck out his hand again. Brady still wouldn't take it. He looked at me.

" 'I didn't get your name, sir?'

" 'Noah Williams,' I said.

"We shook hands.

" 'You stay here with Daddy?'

" 'No, just visitin'. I live in the quarter.'

" 'What kinda work y'all do around here?'

" 'What can you do?'

" ''Most anything.'

" 'Know how to cut grass?'

" 'Everybody knows how to cut grass.'

" 'You can make some pretty good change—cuttin' grass.'

"That boy looked down on me like I had hit him.

" 'Me?' he said, and tot his chest. 'Me? Cut grass?'

" 'With a mowing machine, you can make some pretty good change—enough to feed yourself.'

" 'Any other kinda work around here? I need money.'

" 'You can ax around.'

"He turnt back to Brady.

" 'Daddy, can I stay here couple days?'

"Brady didn't answer him, like he didn't know he was still there. I tot Brady on the knee, and he looked up at the boy.

" 'Can I stay here couple days?'

" 'Room over there. You got to clean it out. Sleep there if you want.'

"Boy went to the other door and pulled it open. Sun had gone down, but he could see in there.

" 'Good Lord, it'll take me a day to clean this up.'

"He come on back where we was settin'. He said, 'I'll sleep in my car tonight. Clean it tomorrow.'

"I stayed there with Brady few more minutes, then I started for home. That boy was 'sleep in the car."

Behind me I heard, "I ever told you about that bottle of salt water with three different colors?"

I nodded.

"Liked for me to wash her back. Stick her toes out just 'bove them bubbles—toenails painted red, green, and pink—she wiggle them a little bit. Then she do that other foot—stick her toes out just 'nough for me to see them wiggling; then she duck her foot back in the water. . . . Lord, have mercy, she knows what she do to me—make me want to jump in that tub with all my clothes on . . . And you think I'll let a ugly-ass nigger with a mouth full of cheap-ass gold take her from me—'cause he carry a gun? Shit, I carry a gun too. I can't respect no nigger who don't carry a gun—not in these days—shit."

Jamison was talking again:

"Spent all day cleaning out that room. Had to use shovel, broom, and mop. When he finished, Brady was already sittin' out on the garry smoking his pipe. Boy asked him if he needed anything. Brady didn't answer. Stella said he came in around six o'clock that night and ordered a hamburger and a bottle of beer. Said he needed to make some money. Said he asked her if she needed any help around the place. He could wait on tables, wash dishes, clean up—anything. But she didn't need any help. He went over to Luther, asked Luther if he needed any help in the bar; he could be bartender, he could clean up, he could be bouncer—anything. Luther didn't need no help either. He came back about ten that night; first thing the next morning he was out there again.

"First place he stopped was the store. Will Baptiste was there talking to old Billy Boudreau in Creole. Boy come in.

"Boy: 'You need somebody to do some work?'

"Old Billy Boudreau: 'No.'

"'I can clean up,' the boy said. 'I can move heavy things. Sacks of rice, sacks of flour—I can move things like that for you.'

"'I just have five-pounds sack of rice; same with sacks of flour and sugar. I can move all that with one hand.'

"'I can deliver things after people buy from you.'

"'They buy, they take it with them—hanh, Will?'

"Will Baptiste nodded his head.

"'I can paint the store for you. Looks like it can stand a painting.'

"Will Baptiste told us old Billy Boudreau looked around the store at every wall, even up at the ceiling.

"Said he said, 'Will, you can recall the last time this place have been painted—if ever?'

"Will Baptiste shook his head.

"'Best you look for work someplace else,' old Boudreau told him. 'Who are you anyway?'

"'Brady Sims's boy.'

"Old Billy Boudreau looked him over. 'Oh, yeah, yeah,

I remember now. Y'all went to California? How's that weather out there?'

"'Fine.'

"'Better than here?'

"'Sometimes.'

"'Yeah, yeah, I heard that. Well, best you look for work somewhere else. I don't need help.'

"He leaves the store; next he goes to Mack Bergeron's house. Drive in that front yard, like driving in somebody's front yard in the quarter. Celestine said when she answered that door she nearly fainted.

"'Boy, what you want?'

"'They need anybody to do some work around here?'

"'Boy, ain't you got any better sense than to come up to this front door. What you think that back door is made for?'

"'Just looking for work.'

"'I don't care what you looking for—you look for it at that back door. Now, you better get away from here 'fore Mr. Mack or Miss Joyce come here and catch you and that car in this front yard.'

"She slammed the door in his face.

"He left. He stopped at LeJeune plantation house; he stopped at the store. He went to Henry Riehl plantation house, stop there; went to the store. No, no, no; nobody needed any help. He stopped at the pecan factory. Didn't need any help either. He came into Bayonne. He noticed all the things Jack Trudeau had on the sidewalk—rakes, brooms, mowing machine, a shovel, a hoe—he went in. He asked Jack Trudeau if he needed a clerk, or someone to keep records, or someone just to clean up the place. 'Lloyd Zeno,' said Jack Trudeau, scratching the inside of his ear (like he always do), just looked at the boy.

"Then he said: 'Boy, where—who are you?'

"'Brady Sims's boy.'

"Lloyd said Jack Trudeau nodded for him to come over. Lloyd had been sweeping up the place.

"'Claim he is one of Brady's sons; thought they had all gone to California?'

"'Last I heard,' Lloyd said.

"Lloyd said Jack Trudeau scratch inside his ear again.

"'Where you from?' he asked.

"'California.'

"Jack Trudeau looked him up and down and shook his head.

"'No, I don't need a stock clerk. I'm the stock clerk.'

"'I can move things.'

"'I have two boys to do that.'

"'I can keep things clean around here.'

"'That's Lloyd's job.'

"Lloyd said the boy looked around in the store, then thanked Jack Trudeau and left. Jack Trudeau followed the boy outside and watched him drive up the street. He came back in scratching his ear and talking to himself. 'I don't know what get into some of these niggers these days. Leave from here a few years—come back and want to be clerks. Now, Lloyd, if he had told me he wanted to be my secretary, and he could show me how to save money paying taxes—I woulda thought about hiring him. But, no—clerk.' He scratch his ear again, and Lloyd went back to sweeping the floor.

"Jake LeCoz, Harry Green, and Sam Ferdinand was eating lunch when the boy stopped in front of the gas station. Jake asked him what he wanted. He told Jake he wanted to see the boss. Jake told him he could handle any business he needed. He said he wanted to see the boss. Jake asked him if it had anything to do with the car. He asked Jake if the boss was inside. Jake told him yes, but I wouldn't go in if I was you. He went in. Joe DeLong was on the phone. He didn't look at the boy until he had finished talking. Then he looked at him awhile before he asked him what he wanted.

"'You got any work? I can do mechanic work.'

"'Did you see those boys out there?'

"'I saw them standing 'round eating.'

"'Didn't Jake tell you not to come in here bothering me?'

"'He said something like that, but I—'

"'Get out of here, and don't ever come back in here again.'

"Next place he stopped, Semour drugstore. White people eating at the counter, Edna behind the counter serving, Robert Semour at the cash register. Robert sees him: 'Hey, you looking for something?'

"'You the owner?'

"'I asked, are you looking for something?'

"'Looking for work.'

"'You're in the wrong place. Get out of here.'

"He looked around the drugstore, especially at the white people eating at the counter.

"'You hard on hearing?' Robert said, getting up from his seat behind the cash register.

"He left. Montemare hardware store on St. Louis Street, his next stop. Montemare and two other Cajuns was in there talking in Creole. Joe Lenard was stacking cans of paint in a corner.

"Montemare saw the boy. 'Yeah?'

"'Looking for work.'

"Joe Lenard said Montemare called him. 'Hey, Joe. Boy here says he wants your job.'

"'I need it myself, Mr. Montemare.'

"'Sorry, but Joe says he has to feed his children. Good luck, though.'

"He drove back to Stella, ordered a hamburger and a beer. Stella could tell he was hungry, and she gave him a plate of beans and rice and a piece of stewed chicken for the same price of a hamburger.

"'Still looking 'round?' she asked him.

"'Nothing 'round here a man can do,' he said.

"'Keep trying,' she told him. 'Something bound to come up.'"

Noah Williams started talking:

"Me and Jules Grimmion was sitting on the garry talkin'. I could see the dust coming down the quarter, then the boy stopped the car before the house and came on in the yard. He spoke to us and took a seat on the steps.

"'Found anything?' I ax him.

"'Nothing.'

"He sounded tired.

"'How much you make cutting grass?'

"''Pending how hard you work. With your own tools—twenty, twenty-five dollars in a day.'

"Chocktaw could muster up thirty, thirty-five dollars. Hardworking old boy, 'til that snake caught him on the leg—a cottonmouth."

Behind me I heard: "See what I mean? See what I mean? Now it's Chocktaw and some fucking snake."

"He had his own gear—weed eater—everything."

"Chocktaw had a weed eater," I heard behind me. "Now I have heard everything. The man kills his son with a gun; this old bastard brings up weed eater. Instead of N'Awlens, I ought to head my ass toward Jackson—listening to this shit."

"'A snake bit him?' the boy ax.

"'Cuttin' ditch bank for Cecil Jarreau, and not wearin' boots. Snake caught him jus' 'bove the ankle.'

"'How long do you have to work for twenty-five dollars?'

"'Pretty much the whole day.'

" 'And for a mangy twenty-five dollars?'

" 'They's some cotton picking still left out there.'

"From the steps, that boy looked up at Jules and tot his chest couple times.

" 'Me?' he said. 'Pick cotton? Me?'

" 'Man might do 'most anything if he get hungry enough.'

" 'I don't know if y'all down here have heard it—slavery been over.'

" 'We heard,' Jules said. 'But a man got to do somethin' to eat and put clothes on his back.'

"The boy nodded his head and got up from the steps.

" 'Thank y'all for talking. I'll keep looking around. Good night.'

"Dust followed the car down the road, back in the field.

" 'I hope that boy don't do nothing crazy for money,' Jules said."

Jamison was talking again:

"He worked his way toward Bayonne the first day; now, the next day he went in the opposite direction. Hébert plantation—nothing doing; Samson plantation—same thing; Loddio—nothing; at Pitcher, they told him he could come back at grinding. He went to the old Creole place; they wouldn't even talk to him there. He went to Reese Phillip gas station in Johnsonville. He went to White and Black cafés and bars in Port Alfred—but nothing doing. Noah, you said you didn't know what it was the first time you smelled a reefer?"

Behind me I heard this intake, and this loud exhale of breath.

Noah Williams was saying:

"Sittin' on the garry with Brady that evening, I notice a funny kinda smell. I knowed it wasn't Brady, 'cause he smoked just Buzz tobacco. Hadn't never been 'round nobody smoking reefers before, so I couldn't tell what it was. Brady went on smoking his pipe and looking out at the old sugarhouse. We had been talking 'bout the sugarhouse earlier, when we used to grind cane there; and I s'pose he was still thinkin' 'bout those old days. But me, I couldn't get that reefer smell out my mind. After a while, Jean-Pierre started bringing a woman there. A black one at first. They be in that room laughing and talking and smoking reefers. Then they get on that bed, and you could hear that old spring even out on the garry. Th-bang, th-bang, th-bang, th-bang.

"That one was black; then he started bringing a white one there—one of Alvin Tousaint daughters—not that fine one—that li'l skinny one—that chicken legs one. Laughing and talking and smoking reefers, and then on that bed. And you could hear that old gal, 'Oh, oh, oh, oh.' And that old spring going th-bang, bang, bang, bang—louder and louder. And that old gal gettin' louder and louder and louder—like she and that old spring was racing to see which one could make the most noise. Next time he brought her there, Brady stopped him at the steps. Told him to take her and his clothes 'way from his house. Boy asked Brady where he was go'n stay. Brady told him go stay with her. He asked me if they had any more empty rooms in the quarter. I told him yes, but he had to see Mack Bergeron about that. Slept in his car that night; first thing the next morning, drove up to the house and knocked on that kitchen door. Celestine answered.

"'I see you done found some sense,' she told him.

"'Like to speak to Mack Bergeron.'

"'That's Mr. Mack Bergeron.'

"'Yeah—mister.'

"Celestine said she didn't have to find Mack Bergeron. He had probably seen the car drive up in the yard.

"'Do for you?' he said.

"The boy told him.

"'You and Brady had a round?'

"'Yes, sir.'

"'Sooner or later it happens with Brady.'

"He told him that Arthur Simmons had an extra room in his house. He could go down the quarter and talk to him. Aunt Sis and Uncle Buck had another room. If he found something he liked, it would be dollar a day, thirty dollars a month. If he paid now, he would charge him twenty-five dollars a month. Boy told him he wanted it for a week, and he'll see if he wanted it longer. He gave Mack Bergeron seven dollars and left.

"Arthur Simmons said he didn't mind having li'l company, since Loretta had died and all the children had moved. The extra room was already furnished."

Chapter Seven

———

Now Jamison was talking:

"People started seeing a strange car with a California license plate cruising around at night. They saw it cruising up and down East Boulevard in Baton Rouge only at night. They saw it two or three nights before it stopped and two men got out and came into Jimmy's liquor store. Bert Robillard—you know how he comes into Jimmy's all dressed up. Dressed from head to foot—suit, tie, shined shoes—order that one drink and go outside to drink it. Didn't want to be around those sweaty, noisy niggers inside—would go outside. Goes to two more bars—dressed sharp as a tack—order his drinks and go outside to drink it—every night. He was the first one to notice that strange car; and he was standing outside with his drink when they stopped at Jimmy's. Each one bought a drink—bourbon and water. They asked Jimmy if Louisiana Roy ever came in there. Jimmy told them he didn't know any Louisiana Roy. Jimmy asked some other people in the place if they knowed a Louisiana Roy. None of them ever heard of a Louisiana Roy. They went outside and asked Bert Robillard if he knowed a Louisiana Roy. Bert Robillard shook his head. They drove around and visited every colored bar in Baton Rouge—no, nobody knowed a Louisiana Roy. They crossed the river. In Port Arthur, they asked about a Louisiana Roy. Nope. They found Bar One, went in and had a drink. But nobody there knowed Louisiana Roy either.

"To show you how fate work, that same night Jean-Pierre drove up to Bar One. He had to drive around before he could find a parking space. He started to park his car, but he must've recognized that other car or that California license plate, because he got out of there quick as he could. Jobbo nephew, Plukum, and that crossed-eye sissy from Loddio they called Cuddles was in the car with him—Cuddles in the backseat."

"See what I mean, see what I mean," I could hear behind me. He was talking to himself, but loud enough for me to hear him. "Now a crossed-eye sissy I have to put up with. Boy, you pray to God I never run across you in Natchitoches. I'll make you pay for what I'm missing tonight."

Jamison continued:

"They went to all the colored places in Port Arthur. Nobody ever heard of a Louisiana Roy. He's a tall, dark, brown-skinned fellow, on the slim side? Nope, never heard of him.

"Now they started thinking—maybe there wasn't a Louisiana Roy. Maybe he had made up that name when he came to California. They knew that he was from somewhere around here. Now they started asking people if they knew a family that had gone to California some years back. Many people had gone to California few years back, the people told them. And people started to get suspicious now—who were those two men? Who was this Louisiana Roy?

"Jean-Pierre didn't go out anymore. Stayed in his room. Had parked his car in the backyard. That li'l chicken legs gal brought him food and something to drink.

"That sissy from Loddio, Cuddles, and another sissy from Pitcher quarter used to run around together. One night they dropped in at Bar One, and the two fellows from California happened to be standing at the bar. That crossed-eye sissy—in sissy fashion—said, 'How are you gentlemen tonight? I heard from the grapevine that you two gentlemen are in the avenue of looking for someone? I may be of some assistance.' . . . All this came out in court . . . eh, Felix?"

"Truer words never spoken."

"The two sissies was drinking piña colada—all that came out in court. . . . Right or wrong, Felix?"

"You got it, man."

"'Of course, it'll cost you,' the sissy from Loddio, Cuddles, said.

"'How much?' the one who got kilt said. He did all the talking. Lawton something, or something Lawton—I know that Lawton was part of his name. The other one was called Fee.

"'I'll be reasonable,' the sissy said.

"'Go on,' Lawton, the one that got kilt, said.

"'What's the matter with your friend there? Seems like the quiet type. I bet you he can be dangerous.'

"'Oh, Cuddles, stop it,' the other sissy said. 'You some crazy.'

"'Go on,' Lawton said. 'If it's the right product, you'll be paid well. Your friend, too.'

"'Oh, listen to him brag,' the crossed-eye sissy said.

"The other one patted him on the shoulder again. Them li'l sissy pats—with just the tip of your fingers—not your whole hand.

"'Cuddles, you some crazy,' he said, in sissy fashion.

"All that came out in court. Them two sissies were dressed to kill—silk slacks, silk shirts, opened collars, silk sport jacket—and you could smell that perfume all over the courtroom.

"Judge Reynolds took off his glasses, blew his breath on them, and wiped them with a Kleenex. All the while he was looking at both—that sissy from Loddio and Brady's boy from California. Even when he was putting the glasses back on he was looking at them. He took out a little silver snuff case, drew snuff in each nostril, and made a little quiet cough.

"'God bless,' the Loddio sissy told him.

"He nodded, and told the sissy to go on.

"'I asked him had he considered looking down country roads least traveled—like plantations? He hadn't. I told him to try it sometime. And I told him that he didn't have to go any farther west than Bayonne. And I told him, by the way, I have friends who knows how to deal with people who don't pay up. And I turned to Elly—sitting right over there—his name is Elliot—but we all call him Elly—I said, Elly, service, please. Didn't I, Elly?'

"'Elly doesn't have to answer,' the judge said. 'You're excused.'

"'Oh, I can stay longer, if my service is needed.'

"'You're excused, I've heard all I need to hear.' That sissy got up from his chair, bowed and thank the judge, then he waved to his friends in the courtroom and blew a kiss.

"And if I'm lying, I'm flying. Where you at, Lucas?"

"The truth in every word," Lucas said.

"Lord, have mercy," I heard behind me. He was talking to himself. "I want to understand. I really want to understand. I want You to help me understand."

Jamison never stopped talking:

"They started at Pitcher quarter. 'A tall, dark, brown-skinned man in his midtwenties?' Nobody at Pitcher ever heard of him. They went to Loddio. 'Nope.' Bergeron, Samson, Hébert, LeJeune, Riehl—'Nope, nope, nope, nope.' They didn't know anybody with that name. They knew couple of Louisiana Slim, couple of Louisiana Red—but no Louisiana Roy.

"But they had a strange feeling when they got to Bergeron—the one who lived told the court. That old fellow at Bergeron—Arthur Simmons—seemed to be hiding something. He looked nervous. They came back, parked on the highway, facing the quarter. That same night that l'il chicken legs white gal brought him some food. They turned down the quarter, lights out, and parked. They saw her go in the yard, and they were pretty sure it was the same place where the old man lived. They sat there and waited.

"Arthur Simmons said he could hear the boy and that little gal in the other room, laughing and talking while he ate his food. Then they lit up a reefer, and the next thing they was on that bed, and that little gal was slamming her leg against that wall like she was trying to tear it down. He said he had heard them on that bed before, but nothing like tonight. When it was over, both of them was breathing hard.

"'What you want tomorrow night?' she asked him.

"'Same thing I want every night, but you can bring me some fried chicken, too,' he told her.

"She left. She drove by them sitting in the car in the

dark. After she had turned on the highway, they drove down to the house, lights still off. One stood by the steps, and the other one went up on the gallery and knocked on the door—a different door this time. The boy asked who it was.

"The man at the door said, 'Tony.'

"The boy asked, 'Tony who?'

"The man said, 'Tony Young.'

"The boy said he didn't know a Tony Young. He was buck naked. He grab a pair of pants and jump out of the window. The man on the ground had moved to that side of the house, and grabbed him before he could make a step. The one at the door bust inside. Arthur Simmons, in the other room, pressed one ear to the wall. He could hear the man in the yard saying, 'Man, hurry, this nigger is buck naked.'

"'Naked?'

"'He thinks he's a wildcat—biting, scratching, kicking.'

"Arthur Simmons pressed his other ear to the wall. He heard the man in the room saying, 'I got to find some clothes. I don't want one of these rednecks stopping us with a naked-ass nigger in the car.'

"The one in the yard said, 'Just hurry—or I'm go'n have to knock this nigger out.'

"Arthur Simmons switched ears again, and he heard the man inside saying, 'Don't kill him. Too Tall wants his money.'

"'Too Tall ain't trying to hold on to no panther—you sonofabitch, you bit me.'

"'Okay, okay, I've got his clothes.'

"Arthur Simmons said the man inside jumped out of the window. He went to the door and cracked it open, and he could see the two men dragging the boy to the car. They threw him in the backseat, and one of them got in the back with him. The other one swung the car around and they shot out of there.

"Arthur Simmons started running up the quarter, calling: 'Pugg, Pugg—oh, Pugg. Oh, Pugg.'

"Somebody called from one of the galleries: 'What's the matter with you, Arthur? Something done happened?'

"Arthur still calling, 'Oh, Pugg.' Pugg met him in the yard, wearing overalls—no shirt, no shoes. Arthur Simmons out of breath: 'Get on your horse, go tell Brady two men done grabbed his boy.'

"Pugg, just in overalls—no shirt, no shoes—put a bridle on Jacob and headed for the fields. It was dark he said, he could see Brady's head before he could see Brady. Brady was sitting out on the gallery smoking his pipe. Pugg rode up to the gallery.

"'Arthur told me come tell you two men grabbed your boy. Took him in a car somewhere.'

"Pugg said Brady stuffed his pipe with his finger. 'Figgered it was something like that,' he said.

"'What you go'n do?' Pugg asked.

"Brady didn't answer him.

"'You want me go see if I can't get Fifty Cent to take me to see Mapes?'

"'Suit yourself. Long as you pay for it.'

"He stuffed his pipe again. Pugg said Brady acted like he wasn't even there. He said he pulled on the rein, and told Jacob, 'Come on, Jacob, let's go home.'"

Chapter Eight

"They drove down Cobb Road and parked. Brady's son had put on his clothes. The man in the backseat— Lawton something, or—no matter—he said: 'Too Tall Sammy wants his twenty Gs.'

"That boy Jean-Pierre said: 'I never had no twenty Gs. I had ten. Charlie-O had the other ten.'

"The one in the backseat with the boy—the one who got killed—did all the talking: 'We caught up with Charlie-O. He said you kept it all.'

" 'Charlie-O lied. He got half.'

" 'Charlie-O lied?'

" 'If he said I took it all, he lied.'

" 'When a man beg you to hurry up and kill him he's lying?'

"'If he said I took it all, he's lying.'

"All of this came out in court from the one who lived. Where you at, Lucas?"

"Right here with you, man," Lucas assured him.

"'You remember Li'l Jim? You remember what Too Tall Sammy did to him for just misappropriating one G? Not twenty—just one? Made you want to puke—remember? He did twice as much to Charlie-O.'

"'Yeah,' the one under the wheel in front said. 'And Li'l Jim wasn't nothing more than a li'l humpback.'

"The one in back said to the one in front: 'I've told you a thousand times, it's hunch. He was a hunchback. Hunch. You ought to read a book sometime.'

"'Yeah. Hunch. I liked the li'l fellow.'

"'We all liked him. That's why you wanted to puke for the suffering he was taking.'

"All of this came out at the trial. You know how them lawyers like to get to the bottom of things.

"The one in the backseat—the one got killed—said: 'Let's talk about you and Too Tall Sammy's money. Too Tall Sammy wants his twenty Gs, or bring you back alive. I think he has plans for you. Big plans.'

"'I done told you already, I had only ten.'

"'Hand over the ten, and we'll try to figure something out.'

"'I don't have it.'

"'You don't have it? You don't even have half of the money? Don't tell me that you been giving Too Tall

Sammy's money to that little funny-ass-looking white gal?'

"'I lost it gambling.'

"'Am I hearing you right? You've been gambling with Too Tall Sammy's money—and losing?'

"'I was trying to win, and I wanted to come back, and pay him, and ask him to forgive me.'

"'I'm feeling sorry for you already,' the one in front said. 'Too Tall likes to make people watch. I don't want to watch this.'

"'I don't want to see it, either,' the one in back said, 'but it's up to you.'

"'I don't have it.'

"'You want to face Too Tall Sammy?'

"'I don't have his ten grands.'

"'Why do you keep saying ten when I say twenty? You're trying to say I'm lying.'

"'No, but Charlie-O is.'

"'No, baby boy—not Charlie-O—you're the one lying,' he said. And he told the one in front to light up a reefer. He called it a joint. All that came out in court. Lucas was there.

"Say, Luke?"

"Every word you spoke."

"The one in front lit up the reefer and took a long drag on it (all this came out in court) and he passed it to the back, and after Lawton (I'm not sure if it was Lawton something, or something Lawton), anyway after he took his drag, he passed it to the boy. The boy took his drag, and he gave it back to the man in front who held on to it for while before he passed it round again. A matter of fact the one in the back had to reach for it.

"The one in the back with the boy said, 'You wouldn't happen to have a rich daddy, or a rich uncle—or know one of those old southern colonels you-all down here call "Massa"—who would be willing to lend you the money?'

"'I don't know anybody in the world who would lend me ten thousand dollars.'

"'You keep saying ten, and I say twenty.'

"'I don't know anybody in the world who would even lend me twenty dollars.'

"'Not even that little white gal you've been screwing?'

"'What li'l white gal?'

"'Don't play games. We saw her leave the house.'

"'She's poorer than I am. She's been bringing me food.'

"'Feeding you and fucking you too, huh? They pretty generous down here.'

"The one who lived, Fee, said they lit up again. Jean-Pierre stayed quiet.

"'This ain't getting us nowhere,' Lawton said. 'You ready to head back to California?'

"According to Fee, Jean-Pierre sat there mumbling to himself awhile, before he looked up at Lawton.

"'What?' Lawton said.

"'I need some money, too.'

"'All I want is twenty thousand dollars, and let me head back to civilization,' Lawton said.

"'You can't find that kind of money 'round here 'cept in a bank.'

"Fee said Lawton looked at Jean-Pierre a long time. Jean-Pierre looked back at him, then nodded his head. 'The only place.'

"'You ever tried to rob a bank before?' Lawton asked.

"'No. Take more than one person to rob a bank, and everybody 'round here too scared.'

"'You not?'

"'I need money.'

"'And three people can do it?'

"'I think so.'

"'You know anything about this bank?'

"'Just a little old bank.'

"'Where is this bank?'

"'In town. On the main street.'

"'How many people work in the bank? Guards? Clerks? Everybody?'

"'Three or four—that's all.'

"'Guards—with guns?'

"'No.'

"'How do you know?'

"'I been there a couple times. Never seen a guard.'

"'Other people—clerks?'

"'Two clerks—women. Two men in the back office.'

"'How do you know that's all of them?'

" 'I been in there, I looked around. I thought about this.'

" 'Just waiting for help?'

" 'Kind of.'

" 'What you think, Fee?'

" 'I move with the wind, man.'

" 'How far is town from here?' Lawton asked.

" 'Couple—few miles.'

" 'Let's go see that bank.'

" 'Tonight?'

" 'I want to see what it looks like.'

"Ten minutes later they came into Bayonne. They had been quiet all the way.

" 'Drive slow, but not too slow,' Lawton told Fee.

"Jean-Pierre pointed out the bank. Y'all all know what it look like—a little low building settin' between David Hardware and Morgan department store.

"They drove up to the courthouse to turn around, and coming back Lawton told Fee to go slow so he could study the surroundings again. Then they drove out of town, passed the pecan factory, up to Old Cajun Road. They drove about a mile down the road and parked by the ditch. Very few cars drove that old road at night.

" 'We'll sleep here tonight,' Lawton said. 'Fee, you keep the first watch. Keep your eyes on the bank robber. He might change his mind.'

" 'He won't change his mind. He likes robbing banks.'

"Lawton slept until around midnight, then he told Fee

that he'll keep watch. Jean-Pierre slept the whole night through.

"'Where can you wash up around here?' Lawton asked, the next morning.

"'The river back 'cross the highway. They got a bathroom at the courthouse for colored to use.'

"'Yeah, you would like for us to go to the courthouse, wouldn't you?' Lawton said.

"He told Fee to get his shaving kit and food out of the trunk. Fee brought the stuff, and a large Coke bottle of water. Lawton poured water in his hand from the bottle and washed his face and dried it on a handkerchief. Jean-Pierre and Fee did the same.

"Lawton passed out ham and cheese sandwiches. (All of this came out in court.) They ate and drank water from the big Coke bottle. After they finished eating it was piss time. They got out of the car and peed in the ditch. Back in the car, Lawton told Fee to light up again.

"'What time this famous bank opens?' Lawton said.

"''Round ten.'

"'Yeah, everything down here moves slow and late,' Lawton said. 'We'll leave at ten—don't want to be the first ones in the bank.'

"Lawton told Fee to give him the package. Fee reached under the passenger seat and brought out a little leather sample case. Lawton snapped it open and studied the guns. Must to had four or five different guns in there. Couple automatic pistols, couple revolvers. He looked them over. Fee said he watched Jean-Pierre's face. He said Jean-Pierre started sweating. He said Lawton checked a revolver and handed it to him. He checked it again to make sure it was loaded. Lawton stuck one of the automatic pistols under his belt. He snapped the case shut.

"'We are ready if any of those honkies stop us. You'll get yours when we get to town. I don't want you to get anxious. It's five 'til, let's go.'

"It was five after ten when they came into Bayonne. Lawton told Fee to drop him and Jean-Pierre off a half block before reaching the bank. He gave Jean-Pierre the revolver and told him to put it in his pocket before he got out of the car. He told Fee to turn the car around, headed out of town. Him and Jean-Pierre got out and started walking, just casually. Only one customer was in the bank and he was leaving.

"'What can I do for you boys?' the little clerk asked them.

"Lawton said: 'If you make a sound I'll kill you.' He leapt over the railing. 'How much money you got in that draw'?'

"'Not much.'

"'Keep your hands where I can see them,' he told the little clerk.

"He stuck his gun in her back and told her to go to the office door and knock softly. If she tried to make any sign, he told her, he would kill her as sure as hell. She knocked softly, and they went in. Ted Morgan, president of the bank, was at his desk. The other clerk who worked up front was talking to Leigh Melacon at his desk.

"'Any crazy movement—any—I'll kill every one of you. One of you get up and open that safe—no monkey business—I want twenty thousand dollars.'

"Ted Morgan, with his hands over his head, stood up and went to the safe.

"'Don't bring anything out of the safe but money—I mean it. I'll kill every last one of you.'

"That li'l clerk who had been talking to Leigh Melacon turned red as a beet and went down on the floor. Lawton took his eyes off Leigh for no more than a second, but that was enough time for Melacon to reach for his gun. He and Lawton must have fired at the same time. Melacon's bullet caught Lawton; Lawton's bullet caught that li'l clerk in the back. The clerk fell, Melacon kept on shooting. Lawton stumbled out of the office reaching out to Jean-Pierre to help him. Melacon came out of the office, still shooting. Jean-Pierre shot once, hit nothing, dropped the gun, and started running.

"Fee had heard the shooting, and headed out of town. Jean-Pierre hollered for him to stop, but Fee drove even faster. The people came out of the stores and offices, calling for the police and pointing. One of Mapes's deputies caught up with Fee just after he had passed the pecan factory. Two white men in a pickup truck saw Jean-Pierre coming toward them. By the way he was running from uptown, they figured he had done something wrong. They stopped the truck, and both men jumped out and grabbed him, and held him against the truck until one of Mapes's deputies showed up.

"Lawton was dead. Both Fee and Jean-Pierre was sentenced to sit in Gruesome Gertie's lap. Brady cheated the chair out of one, when he killed his own boy."

Part Two

MAPES

Chapter Nine

Bunch of vultures—look at them. Just look at them. If either one of them puts a mike or a camera in my face, I'll throw him in jail just as sure hell is hot. Look at them— you think they care? Bunch of vultures. To them—"Just another old nigger gone crazy." That's how they see him—"Just another old nigger who has lost his mind." I suppose there'll be twice as many here when I get back. They can't wait to see him in handcuffs.

The sky is blue, the river is calm. Look at how they wave to one another, skiing behind the boats. Free, free, with no cares in the world. It's a beautiful day, sunny and bright—except in my heart. It's dark. His skin is black, mine is white—and he's my friend. I've never known a better man, white or black, than him. Why? Why? Why did you do it? Hell, I know why. I damned well know why.

These on this side of the road, across from the river, sitting in their stately rockers—their servants standing by to pour water, or coffee, or any alcohol they want to drink—they know why. Masters, mistresses, servants, all know him—they all know Brady Sims. Those skiing on the river are too young to know Brady Sims, but these on this side of the road know him—hated him, loved him, respected him, feared him—black and white alike. Hell of a man, that Brady Sims.

"I know you like hunting. Would you like to go with us sometime?"

"Who's us?"

"A club I belong to—five of us."

"You go'n make me a member of that club."

I didn't know how to answer him.

"You better go talk to your people first," he said.

"You kidding, Mapes?" George asked. "Did you tell him sometimes we go out three or four days? And he eat and sleep with Emmett and Taylor?"

I went back. "They say you can hunt with us, if you don't mind eating and sleeping with Emmett and Taylor."

"Any other member of that club got to sleep with Emmett and Taylor?"

"No."

"De's your answer."

I told them.

"And you didn't knock the shit out of him?"

"No. Because he would have hit me back. Then I would have had to kill him. Well?"

"I don't care one way or the other," Harry said.

"Same here," Shelly said.

"Oh, fuck," George said.

"I'm going to hunt with him," I said.

"We're all part owner of that cabin, Mapes," George said.

"I won't use the cabin."

"If it means that much to you, I'll go along—until he says something smart to me. But you told Benny Lopes?"

I told Benny Lopes.

"You've gone fucking crazy, Mapes? Your grandpa and your pa must be turning over in their graves. Your family has been sheriff of this parish since the end of the Civil War—for a hundred years. You want to bring that to an end?"

"Isn't that up to the people?"

"Sure—up to the people—until I tell them what a hundred-percent nigger lover you've become."

"The others don't seem to mind as much as you."

"I see why Shelly would go along—he likes black pussy much as you do. For George and Harry, they're so lame-brain they would hunt and sleep with a fucking ape. That black pussy done run you crazy, Mapes—done converted you into a nigger lover? Get the fuck out of my face, stay the fuck away from me. Go back to your black pussy. Me, I like white pussy; always have, always will; and I hunt only with white men, long as they're not a nigger lover. Stay the fuck away from me from now on."

I left the highway and turned down into the quarter. What a difference: leaving a paved road, the calm, beautiful water of the river, well-kept homes, well-kept yards, live oak trees everywhere, every kind of flower you can name. Now this—a long dirt road, weatherworn shacks on both sides have not been painted in over fifty years; most yards are bare of grass and flowers; you sweep the yard with the same broom you sweep the porch. Chinaberry trees in some of the front yards; pecan trees in the back. A little vegetable garden beside the house; on the porch a wire clothesline stretches from one post to another. A shirt here, a pair of long johns there, a sheet— maybe two sheets on another line at another house. I've been down here many, many times. They all know me. Knew my daddy, who was sheriff before me. Some can even tell you things about my grandpa. "You look like him a lot—but he was more on the lean side."

They're watching me as I drive down the road, driving slow to keep down the dust as much as I can. There is Mister Big Shot—his mon is black, his pa is white, and he calls himself an arsh. He can't say "Irish"—arsh—to distinguish himself from the rest of the blacks in the quarter—arsh. Oh, how he'd like me to stop and pick him up to help me arrest Brady Sims—wouldn't he? I

nod to him, he waves back—a slight wave. I drive slow.
They know why I'm here. They don't need no telephone,
Indian smoke signals, or African tom-tom drums to
hear the news. All they have to do is stick their heads
out the window or out the door and it's right there. . . .
There is the child-breaker—according to rumor, once
you make twelve she'll take you on. She's in her late sixties now, and she's been at it since her teens. Grandpa,
pa, son, grandson—they've all met her over the past fifty
years. . . . The little white church with its blue door and
blue window frame, built by the blacks here on the place,
according to my daddy. I've been in several times to listen to the singing and the praying. . . . They watch as I
go by driving slow to keep down the dust. All that is left
are the old, the very young, and the lame. The old ones
nod and raise their hands to acknowledge my passing;
the children keep on playing. . . . And this one, in her
seventies, light brown skin, still beautiful, has at least a
dozen children by at least a half dozen different men,
black and white.

"Like a dog or a hog."

Daddy grabbed me by the shirt collar and jerked me
toward him, and I hadn't ever seen him so angry before.

"Some people are not as fortunate as you are—always
remember that."

He pushed me away as violently as he had pulled me
to him.

"You and grandpa said it."

"Your grandpa and I didn't know any better," he said. "Why do you think I keep taking you around with me— so you can get to know people. Not all of us have been lucky in this life. Always remember that—always."

They sit in old chairs—chairs as old as they are; some sit on homemade benches; others sit on the steps. They lean against the wall, they lean against a post at the end of the porch. They watch in silence—barely wave—and they know why I'm here.

I leave the quarter and I go into the field, and I think to myself, "Damn you, Brady Sims; damn you." I drive slow, not to keep down the dust—but in no hurry to arrest him. "Why me, Brady Sims? Why me—to send you to Angola? But I must, Brady Sims; I must. You have killed a man—murdered a man—and murderers must go to the pen. Friend or no friend, I must do my duty. And you must sit behind me, not beside me this time, Brady Sims."

He has seen the dust rising above the cane field quarter of a mile away. I drive up and park under a maple tree less than a hundred feet from his house. He stands on the porch leaning against a post.

"Sport," I say to him.

He grunts.

I take a seat on one of the steps and lean back against another.

"How you feel?"

He mumbles.

The old sugarhouse made of bricks stands before us.

There is cane across from the mill and on both sides of the house. But no grinding here anymore. The cane is taken to another house couple miles farther up the road. But he stares at the house as if he remembers when he and others crushed the cane and made the sugar here.

I notice a shovel against the porch with fresh dirt on the blade. What has he been doing for the two hours he needed—digging a grave? Proud as he is, he doesn't want anybody to have to do anything. Is that dirt from a grave?

Far across the field, I can hear the tractor of the St. John brothers as they harvest the cane. Is he listening to it and remembering when there wasn't a tractor, but man and mules hauling the cane to the mill? That was grinding; this is not grinding; when man used his muscle to do all the lifting and hauling—that was grinding. Is that what he is thinking?

I go on talking. He grunts. I talk about the days of hunting together, especially the last time. Emmett and Taylor had stewed some meat with onions and carrots and Irish potatoes. And there was cornbread and mustard greens—and Shelly brought out a half gallon of good red wine, and we all poured some in our tin cups. Even Emmett and Taylor took some back to their tent. But, him? No. "I don't touch that stuff," he said. "Water good 'nuff for me."

We drank. Emmett came back. "Taylor said if you don't mind, can you spare just a li'l touch mo'?"

Shelly filled both tin cups. Emmett said, "Thank you,

suh," three or four times as he backed out the cabin. Shelly told Emmett how good the food was. We all agreed. Brady grunted.

"Only thing would make this better, if we had three or four women back here," Shelly said.

"Shit," George said. "Why the hell you think I come back here?"

We all laughed. Brady grunted—a short laugh.

"What you think about that, Brady?" Shelly asked.

"I never mix 'em."

"Same here," George said. "One, I throw down on the bed; the other one, I throw in the back of my pickup."

"You throw which one where?" Shelly asked.

"Fuck you, Shelly," George said.

We laughed. He grunted.

I had brought a bottle of whisky, and we ended the night like that.

Now, I look at Brady leaning against the post. The shadows of the trees and the house are getting longer by the minute, as the sun slips down slowly beyond the old sugarhouse. What is he looking at? Seeing what? Thinking about what? It is time to go.

"Ready, sport?"

"Give me two minutes."

I had given him three hours. Two more minutes wouldn't matter. While looking down at the ground he takes a long, deep breath; then he raises his head and looking at the old mill and across the fields he does the same—a long, deep breath like he wanted to take in everything for the last time. Then he turns—

And I should have known. Even before I heard it, I should have known. Yes, I should have known. Why? Because I knew Brady Sims.

When I get to the door, I stop. He is lying across the bed. When I see what was left of his face, I turn to find a post I can hang on to and I try to puke my guts out.

Part Three

LOUIS GUERIN

Chapter Ten

The telephone rang. Lucas Felix answered.

"Your boss."

He handed me the phone.

"Yeah?"

"Where the hell have you been? I've been calling all over the place for you."

"Been here at the barbershop, getting a human interest story."

"Do you have a television there?"

"Yeah."

"On?"

"No. Off."

"Turn it on quick. Mapes's about to speak. Your boy

killed himself. Listen to Mapes, then get your butt up here pronto."

I hung up the phone.

"Turn the television on quick. Brady killed himself. Mapes's about to talk."

Sam Hebert snapped on the little black-and-white TV on a shelf above the water fountain. Lights from parked automobiles showed a crowd in front of the courthouse. Mapes and one of his deputies came out and stood before the opened door.

"Watch them lights," Mapes said. "Don't put them lights in my face."

Camera lights were lowered.

"And quiet," Mapes said. The crowd calmed down. "No way that I could have prevented this from happening—no way. I sat on one of the steps to the porch, he leaned against a post not far from me. We talked for about an hour. We talked mainly about hunting together. Then I told him it was about time we started back. He asked me for two minutes to look things over. He wanted to take a last look at everything. Then he went inside and lay down on the bed. When I heard the shot—I got up fast as I could, but I got no farther than the door. No way can I describe what the side of his face and his head looked like. It was the same gun he had used to kill his son earlier today." His voice broke. The crowd remained quiet. "He was a man some people would say was too hard. He lived in hard times—and the burden we put on him wasn't easy. Yes, we. That includes myself. If we had done more, his burden wouldn't have been so heavy.

"I'm going to miss him. You're going to miss him. When he couldn't hunt anymore, he raised a garden. Just as he gave all the meat away that he killed, he gave everything away from his garden. . . . A hell of a man—Brady Sims. Brady Sims—a hell of a man. . . . He was my friend, and one of the best hunters I've ever known.

"Well, that's it. No questions. I'm tired. Talk to you tomorrow. Good night."

In the barbershop we were quiet for a while, lost in our own thoughts; then Jamison said, "I wasn't surprised. Can you see Brady in the pen? Not Brady. Not Brady Sims. That's why he killed that boy; nobody was going to tie a child of his down in no white-man electric chair. And he wasn't going to no pen, either. No, I wasn't surprised a bit."

The old men began to leave the barbershop slowly, quietly. The feller from Natchitoches and I were the last ones to leave, except for Lucas Felix and Sam Hebert.

"Well, partner—by the way, what is your name?"

"Jack Burnet. And you?"

"Louis Guerin," I said. "Which way you're headed?"

"N'Awlens. I'm go'n find that big fine woman no matter where she at, no matter who she with. I'm go'n get down on my knees and say, 'Take me back, baby; take me back, please. I'll be good from now on.'"

"She will."

"You think so?"

"Once you tell her what happened here today, she'll take you back. I'll bet on it."

"If she do, I'm go'n find you one just like her. You can't beat them Creole women for cooking, dancing, and— well, you know the rest. I don't have to mention that." He winked his eye twice.

We shook hands.

"Well, I better hurry and get uptown if I want to keep my job. Take it easy."

"Be seeing you," he said.

Behind us, Lucas Felix was turning out the lights in the barbershop.